First published in Great Britain in 1982 by
Hodder and Stoughton Ltd under the title
More Goodnight Stories

This edition published in 1986 by
Treasure Press
59 Grosvenor Street
London W1

ISBN 1 85051 119 5

Printed in Hong Kong

Enid Blyton

GOODNIGHT STORIES

Illustrated by Suzy-Jane Tanner

TREASURE PRESS

Contents

Jinky's Joke

Once there was a wicked little pixie called Jinky. He was always playing jokes on people, and sometimes they were funny, but more often they were not.

One week he went to all the shops that sold pails and saucepans and ordered dozens to be sent to old Dame Cooky. Well, the poor old lady couldn't *imagine* why so many saucepans and pails kept arriving, and she really grew quite frightened when she saw her kitchen piled up from floor to roof with them. It took her two whole days to take them back to the shops and explain that she hadn't ordered them.

Another time, Jinky put glue on the big wooden seat that stood outside the town hall. People sat there when they waited for the bus. Oh dear, how angry everyone was when the bus came by and they got up—because they left half their skirts behind them!

Now one day Jinky found a few tins of paint as he passed the builder's yard. He tucked them under his arm with a grin. He meant to borrow some of that paint.

He stole into Mother Creaky's back-garden and called her hens to him. He painted those poor hens with the paint out of the tins till they looked like feathered rainbows!

"Oh, Henny-Penny, you do look queer!" said Jinky, laughing as he set free a hen with a red beak, a yellow comb, a purple tail, green wings, and blue legs. And certainly the hen did look very strange. All the other hens looked at her, and then they ran at her and began to peck her, for they thought she was a stranger.

One by one, Jinky painted all the poor hens, and left them squabbling and pecking one another, for they couldn't bear to see such strange-looking creatures. Then Jinky heard Mother Creaky coming, and he hid behind the fence and watched.

"Oh! What's this I see?" cried Mother Creaky, in the greatest astonishment, when she came to her gate. "Are these hens—or are they parrots or kingfishers? Never did I see such colours in my life!"

"Cluck, cluck, cluck!" said the hens sadly, and they ran to their mistress. They rubbed against her skirt and made it red, blue, green, orange, yellow, and purple.

"Oh, you poor creatures!" she cried. "Someone has painted you! You'll all have to be bathed."

Well, of course, hens hate the water, and Mother Creaky got pecked and scratched when she tried to get the paint off their feathers. She heard Jinky chuckling behind the fence, and caught sight of him running away. She was very angry.

"So that's Jinky again, is it?" she grumbled. "Well, it's time he got a fright. He's left behind these paints—and I'll just go along to his house and do a little painting myself. I know he goes to supper with Higgle to-night. I shall have nice time before he goes home."

So Mother Creaky picked up the tins of paint and went along to Jinky's cottage. The front door was black, with a letter-box and a knocker above it. Mother Creaky set to work.

She painted a big face! The letter-box was the mouth, and she painted that red. The knocker was the nose, and she painted that pink. She painted in big eyes and eyebrows and bright yellow hair and a witch's hat above it. When she had

finished, it looked exactly like a witch's face looking down the path. Mother Creaky laughed and hid behind a bush.

The night came and the moon shone out brightly. Jinky came home, whistling, laughing whenever he thought of Mother Creaky's hens.

He turned in at his gate—and then he saw the painted face looking at him from his front door!

"Owwwwww!" cried Jinky in fright. "Ooooooh! Owwwwww! What is it? What is it?"

Then Mother Creaky spoke in a deep voice from behind her bush. It seemed to poor Jinky as if the face on his door were speaking, and he listened in fright.

"Jinky!" said the deep voice. "How dare you play tricks on my friend, Mother Creaky! How dare you upset poor Dame Cooky! I have come to punish you!"

"Oh, please don't, please don't!" wept Jinky. "I won't play tricks again. I didn't know that Dame Cooky and Mother Creaky had a witch for a friend. Please forgive me."

"I will only forgive you if you promise not to play unkind tricks any more," answered the deep voice.

"I promise, I promise!" sobbed Jinky, trembling so much that he could hardly stand.

"Very well. You may come into your house and I will not harm you," said the voice. But Jinky didn't dare to go in. No— he turned and fled away. He spent the night most uncomfortably in a dry ditch, with beetles and spiders crawling all over him.

And in the morning when he crept back to his house, his front door was just the same as usual! You see, Mother Creaky, with many giggles and chuckles, had washed away the witch's face with turpentine and water.

"He'll think twice before he plays a silly

trick again," she said.

And Jinky did think twice. He didn't tell a single person about the witch he had seen—but Mother Creaky told Dame Cooky, and Dame Cooky told the ice-cream man, and he told me—so that's how *I* know!

The Pantomime Cat

"Mollie! John!" called Mummy. "Where are you? I want you a minute."

The two children were playing out in the garden. They ran in.

"I hear that old Mrs. Jones isn't well," said Mummy. "She can't go out and do her shopping. Now I think it would be very nice if you two children did her errands for her each day till she is better."

"Oh, Mummy, I don't like Mrs. Jones!" said Mollie. "She always looks so cross!"

"And she never gives anyone a penny, or a biscuit, or a sweet, or anything," said John.

"You don't do kind things for the sake of pennies or sweets," said Mummy. "You know that. You do it because it is good to be kind. You like me to be kind to you, don't you?"

"Yes," said Mollie. "We love you for it, Mummy! All right. We'll go—won't we, John!"

They were good-hearted children, so each day at ten o'clock in the morning they ran up the hill to Mrs. Jones's little cottage, knocked at the door and asked her what errands she wanted running.

Mrs. Jones never seemed very pleased to see them, and certainly she never gave them anything, not even a sweet out of her peppermint tin. She was not a very kind old lady and although the children were polite to her, and always ran her errands cheerfully, they thought she was a cross old thing, and were glad when they had finished going to the grocer's, the baker's and the fishmonger's each day.

It was the Christmas holidays, and circuses and pantomimes were in every big town. There was a pantomime in the town where Mollie and John lived too, and children often stopped outside the big theatre and looked at the pictures.

"It's Dick Whittington and his Cat," said Mollie. "Last year it was Aladdin and the Lamp. I do wish Mummy would take us, John."

But Mummy said no, she hadn't enough money for all of them. Perhaps they would go the next year.

"You said that last year, Mummy," sighed Mollie. "I do wish we were rich! I'd love to go every night and see Dick Whittington and his clever cat. A girl I know has been, and she says the cat is ever so big and so funny that she laughed till she couldn't laugh any more!'

"Now it's ten o'clock," said Mummy. "Off you go to Mrs. Jones. You won't have to do her errands much longer because she can walk quite well now. You have been good children to run them so cheerfully."

Off went Mollie and John up the hill. They knocked at Mrs. Jones's door and went in. She was sitting at the table, sewing something with a big needle.

The children looked at it. It was a strange thing she was sewing—like a big, black fur rug—with a cat's head.

"Whatever is that?" asked Mollie, in surprise.

"Always asking questions!" grumbled the disagreeable old woman. "It's the cat skin my son wears in the pantomime. Didn't you know he was the Cat in Dick Whittington this year?"

"Oh, no!" cried both children in delight. "How perfectly lovely!"

"Hmmm!" said Mrs. Jones, snapping off her thread. "Not so very lovely, I should think—nasty hot thing to wear every night for hours on end. Hmmm! Now listen—my son wants this cat costume this morning before eleven, so pop down now straightaway and go to the stage door at the back of the theatre. Ask for Mr. Jones and say you've brought his costume. That's all I want you to do to-day. After this morning I can do all my own shopping, so I won't be seeing you any more."

She wrapped up the parcel and the children sped off. "Mean old thing!" said Mollie. "Never even said thank you to us! I say! What fun to be going in at the stage door of the theatre! We might see some fairies—you know—the ones that sing and dance in the pantomime!"

They soon arrived at the stage door and asked the old man there for Mr. Jones.

"Go up the stairs and knock on the second door on the right," said the old chap. Mollie and John ran up the stone steps and knocked on the second door.

"Come in!" shouted someone—and in they went.

A round, jolly-faced man was sitting in front of a mirror. He smiled when he saw them. "Hallo!" he said. "Have you brought my cat skin? Thanks awfully! I say, are you the two children who have been running errands for my mother all this time?"

"Yes," said Mollie shyly.

"And I guess she never said thank you, did she? Or gave you a penny between you," laughed the man. "She's a funny old thing, but she means well. Have you seen me in the pantomime, dressed up in this cat skin?"

"No, we haven't," said John. "Mummy can't afford to take us this year—but oh, you must look lovely! I wish we could see you!"

"Well, you shall!" said the jolly man, unwrapping the parcel. "You shall have free tickets every night of the week, bless your kind little hearts! That's your reward for being kind to someone who never said a word of thanks! I've some free tickets to give away—and my mother never wants to use them—so you shall have them! Would you like that?'

"Oh, yes!" shouted both the children, their faces red with delight. "Yes, yes, yes! We shall see Dick Whittington—and the fairies—and you—and everything else! Oh, what luck!"

Well, it all came true—they did see the pantomime, every night of the week! The jolly man gave them their tickets, and oh, how they loved every minute of it!

"The cat is the best and funniest of all!' said Mollie and John. "We do love him! And we are proud of knowing him, Mummy! Fancy knowing the pantomime cat! All the other boys and girls wish they were us!"

"Ah! You didn't know you were running errands for the pantomime cat's mother, did you!" said Mummy. "You never know what will happen when you do a kindness!"

12

The Goblin who stole Sweets

Somebody was stealing sweets out of the toy sweet-shop in the nursery! There were twelve bottles of sweets there—and every day some of them disappeared.

"*I'm* not stealing them!" said Teddy-bear.

"And I wouldn't touch *one*," said the golliwog, though he was very fond of sweets.

"Well, someone's stealing them," said the Dutch doll. "And what Janet and Ronnie will say when they find out that their toy-shop sweets are gone, I really can't think!"

"We must find out who is taking them," said the blue rabbit. "They disappear in the afternoons, when the children are out for their walk and we are shut up in the toy-cupboard."

"Well, this afternoon we will take the key of the cupboard away, so that Nanny can't lock the door!" said Teddy. "Then we'll creep out and see who is the thief."

So that afternoon, when Janet and Ronnie had gone out for a walk, and had left the toys in the cupboard, they all crept out and hid in different places in the nursery, so that they might watch for the robber.

The golliwog sat up on the nursery window-sill behind the curtain. He looked out of the window.

"Ooooh!" he said. "It's snowing! There is a white carpet all over the ground. I can see all the way down the hill, and there's snow everywhere. I wish we could toboggan!"

"Sh!" said the blue rabbit. "Somebody is coming!"

And sure enough somebody was! It was a little green goblin, with a long nose and ears, and naughty eyes. He slipped in at the door, and ran to the toy sweet-shop. In a trice he picked up two of the bottles of sweets, and was just going to uncork them when the golliwog shouted at him:

"Stop, thief! You naughty robber! Put down those bottles at once!"

The goblin jumped. He looked round —but when he saw only toys watching him, he grinned.

"Shan't!" he said.

"You jolly well will!" said the teddy, and he rushed at the goblin. But quick as lightning the little green fellow ran to the door and out. He slipped into the garden and ran to the gate. Then, staggering about in the thick snow, he began to go down the white hillside with the two bottles of sweets.

"He's taken two whole bottles!" said Teddy.

"Stop him!" said the blue rabbit.

"How?" asked the Dutch doll, very worried.

"Come on, I'll show you!" yelled the golliwog suddenly, and with one leap he was down from the window-sill. He caught up the tin nursery tray and rushed outside, followed by all the rest of the toys. They ran to the gate quite easily, for the snow had been swept away from the path.

"But how can we get down this snowy hill?" asked the Dutch doll, in dismay.

"That's what I brought the tray for—to get down the hill before the goblin does!" cried the golliwog, and he slammed the tray on the snow at the top of the hill. "Get on, everyone."

They all got on, though the blue rabbit was very much afraid. The golliwog gave the tin tray a push and leapt on at the back. The tray slid down the hill.

Whooooooosh! What a slide that was! The tray sped on over the snow like a toboggan, and carried all the toys with it. My word, what a pace it went! You should have seen it! The blue rabbit's whiskers were almost blown off.

The green goblin was still staggering down the hill, deep in the snow. The tray sped after him.

"Whoooooooosh!" cried all the toys. "Look out!"

The goblin heard the noise and looked behind him. He gave a yell. The tray was almost on top of him. He tried to jump out of the way, but it wasn't any good.

Bang! The tray hit him in the back and sent him deep into the snow. He disappeared into the whiteness, and all the toys fell off the tray.

"Ooooh!" said the golly.

"I've bent my whiskers," said the blue rabbit.

"Where are those bottles of sweets?" cried the bear. "Oh—here's one."

"And here's another!" shouted the Dutch doll, picking the second one up from the snow."

"But where's the goblin?" asked the golly.

"We'd better dig him out," said the rabbit.

"Look! There are the children coming home from their walk!" cried the teddy. "We must get home quickly before they see us. Never mind the goblin!"

They all scrambled back up the hill, and in at the nursery door. They shook the snow off themselves as best as they could, stood the tray in the corner, and scurried into the cupboard—only just in time!

"I can't think why our toys feel so wet," said Janet, when she opened the cupboard and took them out. "I'd very much like to know what they've been doing!"

Well, if she asked the green goblin, she'd soon know what the toys had been up to. But, dear me, the green goblin was at the bottom of the snow! And there I'm afraid he'll have to stay till it melts. Serves him right, the naughty little thing!

A Spell for a Puppy

There was once a little girl called Joan. She had a great many toys, books and games, almost every one you could think of. You might have thought she would be happy with so many, but she wasn't.

She hadn't the one thing that she really did badly want—and that was a real, live puppy! Her mother didn't like dogs in the house, and would never let her have a puppy, or a kitten either.

"Why do you keep saying you want a puppy to play with?" she often said impatiently to Joan. "You have so many lovely toys. What about your dolls' house? You never play with that now, Joan. Get it out this morning and give it a good clean. Take it out into the garden. It is nice and warm there, and it doesn't matter if you make a mess on the grass."

Joan didn't want to play with her dolls' house. She was not a little girl who was very fond of dolls. She liked running and jumping, she loved animals and birds. She wished she had been a boy. But she was obedient, so she fetched her dolls' house and took it out into the garden. She went down to the hedge at the bottom, where it was sheltered from the wind, for she did not want all the little carpets and curtains to blow away.

She took everything out and cleaned the house well with a wet cloth. She rubbed up the windows, and shook all the carpets. She polished the furniture and put it back again.

It was really a dear little house. There was a nice kitchen downstairs with a sink, and a fine drawing-room and small dining-room. Upstairs there was a little bathroom with a bath and a basin. Three bedrooms opened out of one another, all papered differently, each with their little carpet on the floor.

"It's a pity, I don't like this sort of toy as most little girls do," thought Joan, as she arranged all the furniture. "I wish I did. But people like different things, I suppose—and I do love animals—and I do wish I had one of my very own."

Just then the dinner-bell rang, and Joan went off to wash her hands and brush her hair. She stood the little house under the hedge out of the sun. She meant to go back after dinner and finish cleaning it outside. The front door knocker wanted a polish, and the chimney wanted washing.

But, after dinner, Mummy said she was going to take Joan out to tea, and the little girl was so pleased that she forgot all about the dolls' house out in the garden. She went off with her mother to catch the bus—and the little house was left under the hedge.

When Joan came back it was late and she was sent to bed at once. She snuggled down under the blankets—and then she suddenly remembered the dolls' house!

"Oh dear!" she said, sitting up in bed. "Whatever would Mummy say if she knew I had left my beautiful dolls' house out-of-doors? I really must go and get it!"

She slipped on her dressing-gown and went down the stairs. She went out of the garden door and ran down the path. There was a bright moon and she could see everything quite clearly. She went to the hedge—and then she stopped still in the greatest surprise!

What do you think? There were lights in her little dolls' house—and people were walking about in the rooms—and the front door was wide open!

"Whoever is in there?" thought Joan, in great excitement. She bent down to see—and to her great delight she saw that the little folk inside were pixies with tiny wings. They were running about, talking at the tops of their voices. They sounded like swallows twittering.

Joan looked into one of the bedrooms through the window—and she saw, fast asleep in one of the small beds, a tiny pixie baby. It was really too good to be true. The little girl sighed with delight—and the pixies heard her!

They slammed the front door at once—and one of them opened a bedroom window and looked out.

"How kind of you to let us have it," said the pixie, beaming all over her little pointed face. "Can't we do something for you in return? Isn't there anything you want very much?"

"Well, yes, there is," said Joan. "I want a puppy dog very, very much. I have wanted one for years. But I have never had one."

"We'll give you a spell for one," said the pixie. She ran downstairs and opened the front door. She held up a very small box to Joan. "Take this," she said. "There is a spell inside. Blow it out of your window to-night and say: "Puppy, puppy, come to me. Make me happy as can be. Puppy, puppy, come to me!"

"Oh, thank you!" said Joan, more excited than ever. "Listen, pixie. Don't you think I'd better take your house to the woods to-morrow? The gardener often comes down here and he might be cross if he saw I'd left my house in the hedge."

"Who are you?" they cried to Joan.

"I'm the little girl this house belongs to," said Joan. "I've been cleaning it to-day, and I left it here and forgot it. What are you doing here?"

"Oh, we found it and thought it would do so nicely for us and our family," said the pixie, in a disappointed voice. "You see, we lived in a nice hollow tree—but the woodmen came and cut it down—and we hadn't a home. Then we came along by your hedge and saw this lovely house. It's just the right size for us, and as there didn't seem to be anyone living in it, we thought we'd take it."

"Well, I simply love to see you in it," said Joan. "I do really."

"Would you let it to us?" asked the pixie. "We would pay you rent, if you liked."

"Oh, no," said Joan. "I don't want you to pay me for it. You can have it, if you like. I am very lucky to see you and talk to you, I think. I am most excited, really I am!"

"Yes, that's a good idea," said the pixie. "We would like to be somewhere in the woods. Will you carry the house there to-morrow morning? We'll show you where we'd like it."

"Yes, I will," promised Joan. "Now, I must go. Good night, and thank you very much."

She ran off, looking back to see the little windows of her dolls' house lighted up so gaily. She went up to her bedroom and opened the small box. She took out the spell, which was like a tiny bit of thistle-down, and blew it out of the window.

"Puppy, puppy, come to me. Make me happy as can be. Puppy, puppy, come to me!" she whispered.

Then she got into bed and fell fast asleep.

And whatever do you think happened next morning? Why, her Uncle Joe came to stay, and with him he brought a small, fat, brown puppy in a basket—a present for Joan!

"Here you are!" he said to the delighted little girl. "I know you've always wanted a pup—and you shall have one! His name is Sandy—treat him well, and he'll be a good friend to you!"

Joan was full of joy. She loved the puppy, and it licked her nose and hands, pleased to have such a nice little mistress. She raced down to the bottom of the garden with the puppy at her heels. The dolls' house was still there, and outside stood all the pixies, waiting for her to come.

"I've got my puppy, I've got my puppy!" she said, joyfully. "The spell worked! Now, I'll carry your house to the woods!"

She picked it up and carried it off, the pixies half flying, half running in front to show her the way. She put it down in a little glade by the side of a small stream and said good-bye once more. Then she and Sandy raced home again, a very happy pair.

And if you should happen to come across a dolls' house in the woods, don't touch it, will you? It will be the one belonging to the pixies! They still live there, you see!

"I have pecked a hole!" he sang, "I have pecked a hole!"

Then a big blackbird fluttered down and put his head inside the hole.

"There is a bun inside!" he sang, "a bun, a big currant bun!"

A thrush joined the little crowd and he pecked at the bun. "It is good!" he said. "I shall eat it. It is mine."

"Yours!" cried the robin, indignantly. "What do you mean? I saw the paper bag first!"

"But I told you there was something inside the bag!" chirrupped the sparrow, at once. "I did, I did!"

The chaffinch pushed against the thrush.

"Go away!" he cried. "This is my bun. It was I who pecked a hole in the bag."

"But I peeped inside it!" said the blackbird. "The bun is mine. Go away, everybody!"

The Birds and the Bun

There was once a baker's boy who went down Leafy Lane with a basket of bread and buns. As he went he sang a song and swung his basket, and out dropped a bag with a large currant bun inside. The boy did not see the bun falling and he went on his way. The bun lay in the lane in its paper bag, and as no one came by that way it stayed there for a whole hour.

Then a robin came by and saw it.

"A paper bag, a paper bag!" he cried.

A brown sparrow flew down and pecked at the bag.

"There's something inside!" he chirrupped.

Down flew a fine chaffinch and pecked open the bag.

"You are foolish!" said the thrush, scornfully. "I pecked the bun first—so it is mine. I am now going to eat it!"

Then there was such a noise of quarrelling and chirrupping and singing that no one could hear himself speak. Suddenly there was a loud caw and down flew a large black rook.

"What is the matter?" he said, in his deep voice.

Then everyone told him about the bun in the paper bag.

"And each of us thinks it is his," said the thrush. "How can we settle it?"

"I will settle it for you," said the rook. "Now, you all have good voices. I will hear you sing for this bun, and I will give it to the one who sings the best."

"That is a good idea," cried everyone, for they all thought they had fine voices, even the shrill sparrows.

"Very well," said the rook. "Now please turn round so that you have your backs to me. When I say 'Go!' open your beaks and sing loudly for all you are worth, till I say stop."

So the robin, the sparrow, the chaffinch, the thrush and the blackbird all turned round with their backs to the rook, opened their beaks, and waited for him to say "Go!"

"Go!" he shouted. And then you should have heard the robin's creamy trill, the sparrow's loud chirrup, the chaffinch's pretty rattle of a song, the thrush's lovely notes and the blackbird's fluting. Really, it was fine to hear. They went on and on and on—and they didn't hear the rook tearing open the paper bag. They didn't hear him taking out the bun. They didn't hear him spreading his great black wings and flying off into the next field. No, they went on and on singing, each trying to outsing the rest.

When they were quite tired of singing, they wondered why the rook did not tell them to stop. So the robin looked round—and he saw that the rook was gone!

He hopped over to the paper bag—and it was empty!

"See, see!" he cried. "The bun is gone—and so is the rook! He has tricked us! Oh, the rascal! Oh, the scamp! Now we have lost our bun!"

"And there was plenty there for all of us!" chirruped the sparrow, in dismay. "Why did we make such a fuss? We could each have had some—and now we have none!"

They flew off in a rage—and you may be sure the rook didn't show himself for a day or two! And when he did, and happened to meet the others, he cawed politely, and said: "Really, my friends, you have REMARKABLY fine singing voices! Do let me hear you some other time!"

And you should hear them shout at him then!

22

The Strange Doll

Doreen was very sad. She had a lovely baby doll that could shut its eyes and could say "Mama" quite plainly—and now the doll was broken!

It wasn't really Doreen's fault. She had put it on the table in the kitchen just for a moment whilst she went to get her doll's pram—and Mummy hadn't seen it there. She had put down a tray of dirty cups and saucers, and the doll had fallen off the table.

Crash! Her pretty face broke into pieces, and both her legs broke, too. Doreen was very much upset and cried bitterly.

"Oh, Mummy, can't she be mended?" she asked. But Mummy shook her head. "No, I don't think so," she said. "She is too much broken. I'm afraid I can't buy you another doll just yet, darling, because I really haven't the money. You must wait for your birthday."

"But that's ever such a long time away," said poor Doreen. "Oh Mummy, I shan't have a doll to take out in my pram now!"

Doreen put the broken doll in the toy cupboard. Then she put her pram away —but when she took hold of the handle, she thought she would go down the lane to the farm and back again, even though she had no doll in the pram to wheel along. She would just pretend!

So off went the little girl, wheeling her empty pram. She went right down to the farm and then just turned to go back again.

Just as she turned, she heard a little whimpering noise. She looked round to see where it was. By the side of the lane, huddled under the hedge, was a puppy-dog. He was crying sadly all to himself.

Doreen went over to him. "What's the matter?" she asked. "Poor little puppy-dog, you are unhappy!"

The little dog whimpered again and did not move. "Come along!" said Doreen. "Come along! Don't sit under the damp hedge. Come out into the road and let me see you!"

But still the puppy did not move. So Doreen picked him up gently—and then she saw that he was hurt! One of his legs was bleeding, and he held it up as if it hurt him very much.

"Oh, dear!" said Doreen. "You're hurt! How did it happen? Did a farmhorse kick you—or a motor-car hurt you?"

The puppy whimpered again and licked Doreen on the face. He thought she was a dear, kind little girl. She put him down on the ground and tried to make him walk after her—but he was very much frightened, and would not move a step.

Doreen remembered that dogs have their names on their collars, so she took hold of his pretty red collar and looked at it. On it was printed: "White Cottage, Elmers End."

"Oh, you belong to Mrs. Harrison, who lives at Elmers End!" said Doreen. "Oh, dear—that's a long way away! I wonder if you can possibly get there."

The puppy yelped. He was trying to tell Doreen what had happened. His mistress had driven her car to the farm that morning, and just as she was leaving again, he had jumped out and hurt his leg. Now he was too frightened to do anything at all.

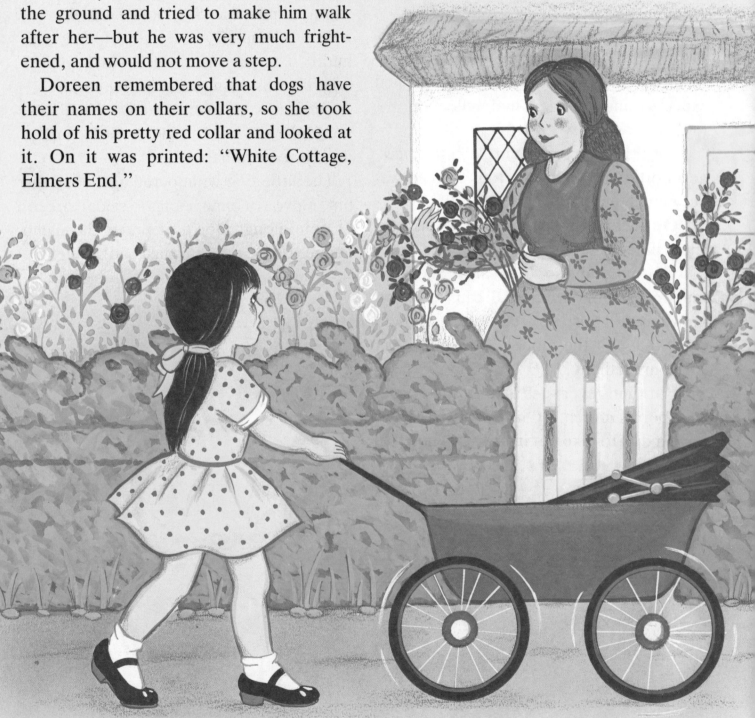

"However can I get you back?" said Doreen, patting the soft little head. "Oh! I've got such a good idea! I'll put you in my doll's pram, puppy! My doll broke this morning, poor thing, and the pram is empty. You'll fit in there nicely, because you are so small. I think I can manage to walk all the way to Mrs. Harrison's."

She picked up the puppy-dog and put him gently into the doll's pram. He snuggled down on the pillow happily. It felt like his soft basket at home! Doreen pulled the covers over him and told him to go to sleep.

And so tired and frightened was the poor little puppy that he really did close his eyes and fall asleep in the pram! Doreen was so pleased.

"It's almost as good as having a doll!" she thought. Off she went, wheeling her pram carefully so as not to wake up the sleeping puppy-dog.

It was a long way to White Cottage where Mrs. Harrison lived. The little girl's legs were very tired long before she got there, but she didn't stop for a moment. She did so badly want to get the puppy back to his home and tell Mrs. Harrison to bathe his leg and wrap it up.

At last she came to White Cottage. Mrs. Harrison was in the garden, cutting roses. She looked up in surprise as she saw Doreen wheeling her pram up the path.

"Good morning, dear!" she called. "Have you come to show me your baby doll? What a long way you must have walked! You look quite tired!"

She went over to the pram and peeped inside—and how astonished she was to see a sleeping puppy there—her own puppy too! She stared and stared!

"Why, it's Sammy!" she said. "I thought I had left him behind at the farm and I was going to fetch him this afternoon!"

"I found him just near the farm, with a hurt leg," said Doreen. "I hadn't a doll in my pram to-day, because it got broken this morning. I was very sad about it because Mummy said it couldn't be mended, and she can't buy me another doll till my birthday. So I took my pram out empty—and it was a good thing I did, really, because, you see, when I found poor Sammy, I could put him into the empty pram and wheel him all the way home to you. I think his leg wants bathing and bandaging, Mrs. Harrison."

What a to-do there was then! The puppy woke up and tried to jump out of the pram when it saw its mistress. Its leg hurt and it yelped. Mrs. Harrison called for warm water and an old handkerchief—and soon the little dog's leg was well bathed and had a nice clean bandage on. He really looked quite proud of it.

"Well, now, my dear, it really is time for your dinner," said Mrs. Harrison, looking at the clock. "Good gracious! It's past one o'clock! Your mother will be worrying about you. I'll run you and your pram home in the car."

She took out her little brown car and popped the pram into the back seat. Doreen sat in the front and in a very little while they were back at Doreen's home. Mrs. Harrison explained to Doreen's mother how kind the little girl had been.

"She tells me her baby doll was broken this morning and that was how it came about that her pram was empty and she could take Sammy back to me," said Mrs. Harrison. "I was so sorry to hear about her doll. Do give it to me, Mrs. White, for I am sure I can get it mended for her. I know a doll's hospital in the next town. I can get a nice new head and two new legs put on, I'm sure."

She took the doll away with her—and will you believe it, in three days she brought it back again—quite better! It had on a lovely new head, just as nice as the first one, and two beautiful fat legs. The doll smiled at Doreen, who hugged it and kissed it in delight.

"Oh, thank you, Mrs. Harrison!" she said. "You are kind!"

"Well, you were kind first!" said Mrs. Harrison, with a smile. "It's funny how things happen, isn't it? Your doll got broken—so you took your pram out empty—and found Sammy and put him into it—and I was pleased, and heard about your broken doll and wanted to get it mended for you! So your bit of kindness has come back to you and made you happy! I'm glad!"

But the gladdest person of all was Doreen as you can guess!

Mrs. Dilly's Duck

Mrs. Dilly had a pet duck. It was large and white and fat, and its name was Jemima. It had a pond all to itself in the garden, and it was very fond of Mrs. Dilly.

One day, when Mrs. Dilly had two friends to tea—Peter Penny and Sally Simple—she told them about her pet duck.

"She's a wonderful creature," she said proudly. "She comes when she's called, and she can shake or nod her head when you ask her questions!"

"Good gracious!" said Peter Penny.

"Call her now," said Sally Simple.

"Jemima, Jemima, Jemima!" cried Mrs. Dilly. The duck was swimming on the pond, but she heard Mrs. Dilly's voice. She swam to the edge, climbed out, waddled down the path and in at the door.

"Quack-quack!" she said.

"Oh, you clever thing," said Peter Penny.

"Do you love your mistress?" said Sally Simple.

Jemima nodded her feathery head twice.

"Do you like worms?" asked Peter Penny.

Jemima nodded her head hard. "Quack, quack, quack!" she said excitedly.

"Would you like to come home with me?" asked Sally Simple.

Jemima shook her head six times. She was much too fond of Mrs. Dilly to want to leave her.

"You're a dear, clever thing!" said Peter Penny, and he held out half of his cake to Jemima. The duck had never tasted cake before and she took it in her beak and gobbled it down eagerly. "Quack!" she said, looking up for more. "Quack!"

Sally Simple gave her a bit of bread and butter with raspberry jam on it. Jemima gobbled it up. Oooh! It was good! Then Mrs. Dilly laughed and held out a ginger biscuit. Jemima gobbled that too. This was better than worms, and better than frogs!

"Now that's enough," said Mrs. Dilly. "Off you go back to the pond, Jemima."

But the duck didn't want to go. It was nice to be made a fuss of, and how she loved the cake and biscuits and bread and butter! She rubbed her soft head against Peter Penny's knee, and he stroked her.

"Do sell her to me any time you are tired of her," said Peter Penny.

"Or to me," said Sally Simple. "I'd love to have a duck like this!"

Mrs. Dilly shooed Jemima out of the warm kitchen and shut the door. "I don't expect I'd ever want to part with her," she said.

Now Jemima the duck had been so excited over her petting and the titbits she had had, that the next day she thought she would go to the kitchen again and see if there were any more treats to be had. So she left the pond and waddled to the kitchen. The door was open. Jemima went in. Mrs. Dilly had just washed over the floor and it was clean and shining. Jemima's feet were muddy and wet. They left dirty marks all over the floor.

Jemima stood on her toes and looked on the table. There was a cake there, just baked. Jemima took two or three pecks at it. It was very good.

Just then Mrs. Dilly came bustling into the kitchen. When she saw her nice clean floor all marked by Jemima's dirty feet she was very angry. But she was even angrier when she saw her new cake pecked to bits!

"Oh, you naughty duck! Oh, you rascally creature!" she cried, clapping her hands at Jemima and shooing her to the door. "Don't you ever do this again!"

But you know, once Jemima had found what a pleasant place the kitchen was, always with something good in the larder or on the table, she used to waddle there every day. Mrs. Dilly tried to remember to keep the door shut, but she hadn't a very good memory, and every time she left it open, Jemima was sure to waddle in!

The things that naughty duck ate! A string of sausages, a cherry-pie, a pound of chocolate biscuits, and even a large cucumber! Mrs. Dilly got crosser and crosser.

"Now, Jemima, the very next time you

come in here, dirtying my kitchen and stealing my food, I shall take you to Peter Penny," she said.

But that afternoon what did she do but leave her door open again, and of course in waddled Jemima and gobbled up a jam tart in the larder!

Mrs. Dilly was very cross. She put on her shawl and hat, tied a string round Jemima's leg, and set off to get the train to Peter Penny's. Jemima was miserable, but she had to go.

Mrs. Dilly took a ticket for herself and one for Jemima. Then she bought a paper and sat down on a seat to wait for the train. She tied Jemima's string to the seat.

Soon, with a roar and a clatter, the train came in. Jemima was frightened and went under the seat. Mrs. Dilly folded her paper, thinking hard about what she had been reading, and ran to the train. She forgot all about Jemima!

She got into the carriage and the train went off. Mrs. Dilly read her paper again. She got out at the next station and set off for Peter Penny's house. Peter was in the garden, working.

"Good-day," he said to Mrs. Dilly. "What have you come along here for?"

"I've brought my duck for you," said Mrs. Dilly. "She's such a nuisance, dirtying my kitchen and stealing food."

"Oh, good!" said Peter Penny, "Where is she?"

Mrs. Dilly looked round for Jemima— but, of course, she wasn't there! She was still in the station!

"Bless us all!" cried Mrs. Dilly. "I've left her by the station seat. How forgetful I am! I must go back and bring her another day."

Well, when she had journeyed back by train to her own station, there was no duck there! Jemima had got tired of hearing trains thundering in and out of the station and had pecked her string in half, Then she had waddled solemnly home, quacking to herself all the way.

When she got back to her garden she had seen that the kitchen door was open as usual. So when Mrs. Dilly arrived back in a flurry, wondering wherever her poor duck had gone to, she found Jemima standing on the kitchen rug, her head tucked into her wing, fast asleep—and the lettuces, tomatoes, and radishes were all missing out of the larder!

"This is too bad, Jemima, too bad!" cried Mrs. Dilly, almost in tears. She took a broom and swept the surprised duck out of the kitchen. "I'll take you to Peter Penny to-morrow as sure as my name is Dilly."

So the next morning Mrs. Dilly tied the string round Jemima's leg once more and hurried to the station. She did not even sit down on the seat this time, in case she forgot Jemima again. She jumped into the train and Jemima had to go too. The frightened duck crept under the seat and lay there whilst the train rumbled on. She was too afraid even to quack.

Mrs. Dilly nodded her head and slept. When the train drew up at the station the porter put his head in at the window and bawled loudly:

"Change here! Change here!"

Mrs. Dilly woke with a jump. She bundled herself out and, rubbing her sleepy eyes, went to the station door to give up her ticket. Then off she went to Peter Penny's.

But she had forgotten Jemima again. The duck was still hiding under the carriage

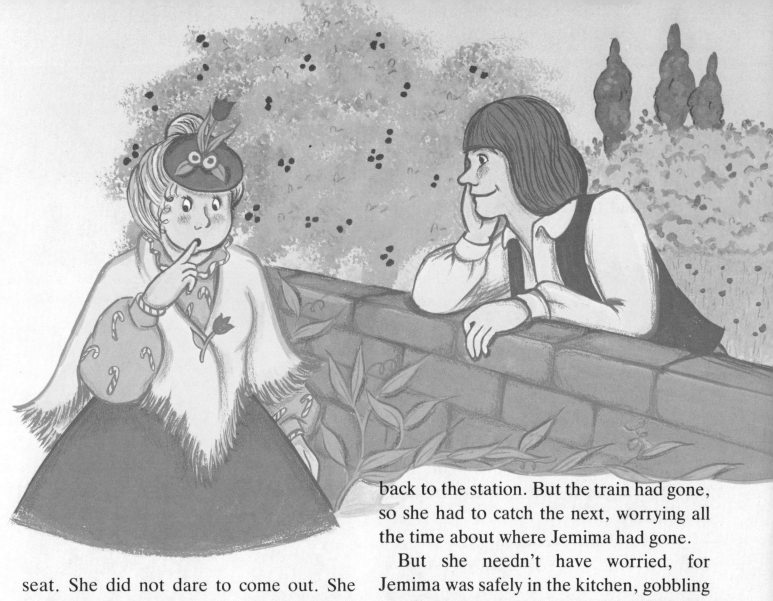

seat. She did not dare to come out. She stayed there till the engine was shunted to the back of the train, ready to go off home once more, for this station was the last one on the line. The train clattered off. When it stopped at Jemima's own station the duck waddled out from under the seat.

Someone opened the door. Jemima jumped out as the passenger was getting in—what a shock he got to see a large duck struggling by him! Jemima gave an anxious quack and waddled out of the station gate. She set off for home.

As for Mrs. Dilly, she soon arrived at Peter Penny's again. "I've brought Jemima as I promised," she said.

"Good!" said Peter Penny. "Bring her in." But there was no duck there to bring in!

"Lawkamussy, I've left her in the train this time!" said Mrs. Dilly, and she hurried

back to the station. But the train had gone, so she had to catch the next, worrying all the time about where Jemima had gone.

But she needn't have worried, for Jemima was safely in the kitchen, gobbling up all the flowers our of the vases. Really, you never knew what that duck was going to eat next!

When Mrs. Dilly got home she was very angry indeed. "I'll take you to Sally Simple's this very afternoon!" she scolded. "I don't like to go to Peter's again, for he will laugh at me—but I'll take you to Sally's and leave you there, as sure as there is butter on bread!"

So that afternoon once more Jemima had a string tied to her leg and once more she set off down the road, this time to Sally Simple's. They didn't go by train, because Sally's was not very far away. They went through the park, where the children were playing, Jemima following solemnly, waddling on her flat feet.

Mrs. Dilly's shoe-lace came undone. She stopped near some railings, and tied

Jemima's string there. There were other strings tied there too—the strings of kites flying high in the air. It was a windy day and the children in the park had brought out their kites. Once they had them high in the air they had tied the strings safely to the railings, so that the kites might fly high, whilst they went off to play ball.

Mrs. Dilly tied up her shoe. Then she untied a string from the railing and set off. But dear old Mrs. Dilly didn't look to see that her string was the right one—and she had untied a kite-string! So off she went, very solemnly, with a kite flying high in the air behind her! How everyone stared!

Sally Simple lived just near the park. Mrs. Dilly went down a street, still flying the kite without knowing it, and knocked at Sally's door.

"Who's there?" cried Sally. "I'm just doing my hair." "It's Mrs. Dilly," said Mrs.

Dilly. "I've brought my bad duck to you. I don't want her any more."

"Bring her in, then—bring her in," said Sally, and she opened the door, with her hair down her back. How she stared when she saw the kite flying behind Mrs. Dilly.

"Why are you flying a kite?" she asked.

"I'm *not* flying a kite!" said Mrs. Dilly, amazed. She looked round for Jemima— and to her enormous astonishment saw that the string went up into the air!

"It must be that Jemima has flown up high in the sky," she said, pulling at the kite. "It can't be a kite, Sally. It must be Jemima flying up there—and yet she didn't have such a long string."

Sally pulled at the string and the kite came down. "It's a kite, Mrs. Dilly," said

Sally. "Well, it's a funny thing that a duck can turn into a kite, but there it is—it seems to have happened!"

Mrs. Dilly was so puzzled that she didn't even remember to say good-bye. She turned and went home, leaving the kite behind her, where it was found by its owner a little while afterwards. Of course Mrs. Dilly didn't find Jemima in the park, for someone had untied the duck and she had waddled home thankfully. When Mrs. Dilly got home she saw Jemima eating the apples out of the fruit dish.

"It seems that I'm not to get rid of you after all, Jemima," said Mrs. Dilly sadly. "I must put up with you. If only I could remember to shut my back door everything would be quite all right! Oh—I know what I'll do! I'll get a cat—and then you will be too frightened to come into the kitchen any more!"

So she got a big white cat called Snowy, and it sat in front of the kitchen fire and warmed its toes. At first Jemima was much too scared to come indoors—but do you know what she is doing now? She is making friends with Snowy the cat, and in no time at all she'll be into the kitchen again, gobbling up all the food in the larder—and I shouldn't be surprised if Snowy doesn't help her!

Poor Mrs. Dilly! I wonder what she'll do then, don't you?

A Basket of Surprises

When Jimmy's mother went to the Garden Fair at the Vicarage she bought a very beautiful basket. It was large and round and deep, and had a fine, strong handle. All round the basket was a pretty green and yellow pattern. It really was a very fine basket, and Jimmy's mother was pleased with it.

"Now, you are not to borrow this basket for anything, Jimmy," she said to him. "You can have my old one if you want one. This is to be kept for special things, like taking eggs to Granny, or something like that."

Jimmy promised. He was once allowed to take some flowers in the basket to old Mr. White, but that was all. And then one day he wanted a basket to take his trains, signals and lines to his friend's, Billy Brown. He went to find the old basket and it wasn't there. His mother was out and no one was at home except Tibby, the big tabby cat, sitting by the fire.

"Where's the old basket, Tibby?" Jimmy asked her. But she just mewed and sat on by the fire, thinking her pussy thoughts. Jimmy hunted everywhere. There was no old basket to be found at all. Perhaps his mother had taken it.

"Well, I'll have to take the new basket," said Jimmy. "I can't possibly take all my things without a basket."

So he took down the beautiful new basket and packed his things into it. Then off he went to Billy's and had a fine tea and a fine game. Billy begged him to lend him his railway for a day, so Jimmy said he would. He set off home with the empty basket, swinging it by the big handle.

He had to go through the woods on his way home, and as he ran he saw a bird fly into a bush. "Hallo!" thought Jimmy, "There's a nest there. I'll just peep and see. I won't disturb the bird in case it deserts its nest—but I would just like to see if there are any baby birds there."

He pushed his way into the bush, but the bird flew out again and into another bush. Jimmy followed her. He felt sure she must have a nest somewhere. But she hadn't. She was just looking for the caterpillars there.

Jimmy set off home again—but suddenly he remembered that he had put down his basket somewhere. Goodness! Where could it be?

He ran back—but no matter how he looked he couldn't find that basket anywhere! "Oh, dear!" thought Jimmy, as he hunted. "Whatever will Mummy say if I go home without it? I am sure I put it down by the bush I first looked in."

But Jimmy couldn't find the bush! And at last he had to go home without the basket. When he told his mother he had lost it she was very cross.

"You are a naughty boy, Jimmy," she said. "I told you not to borrow my best basket. Now, unless it is found again, you must save up your money and buy me a new one."

"Oh, but Mummy, I'm saving up to buy a railway tunnel!" cried Jimmy, in dismay.

"Well, I'm sorry, dear, but you can't buy your tunnel until you have bought a new basket," said his mother. "You had better go and have another hunt for it."

Poor Jimmy! He went and hunted and hunted, but he could not find that basket! The next day his Uncle Peter came to see him and gave him some money to spend—

but his mother said he was to put it all into his money-box to save up for the new basket. He was dreadfully disappointed. The next morning his mother called him and said: "Have you seen Tibby, Jimmy? She isn't in her usual place by the fire, and she hasn't been in for her breakfast."

"No, I haven't seen her," said Jimmy quite worried, for he was very fond of Tibby. "Where can she be?"

"Perhaps she will come in for her dinner," said his mother. But Tibby didn't. There was no sign of her at all. Jimmy got more and more worried. He had had Tibby from a kitten, and the two were great friends. He did so hope she hadn't got caught in a trap.

"Do you think she has, Mummy?" he asked. "Oh, wouldn't it be dreadful if she had gone rabbiting in the woods and got caught in a trap and nobody was there to set her free?"

"Oh, I don't expect she has, for a moment," said his mother. "She hardly ever goes rabbiting. She will turn up, I expect. Now, what are you going to do this afternoon, Jimmy? You said you wanted to go and play with Billy Brown."

"Well, I did want to," said Jimmy. "But I think I'll just go and hunt for Tibby, Mummy. I do feel unhappy about her, really I do."

"After tea we will catch the bus and go into the town to buy a new basket," said his mother. "I really must have another. I think you have enough money in your box now to buy me one."

Jimmy went off to hunt for Tibby, feeling very miserable. "I've lost Tibby, and I've got to give up my railway tunnel and buy a new basket instead," he sighed, as he ran along to the woods. "What a lot of bad luck all at once!"

He soon came to the woods, and he began hunting about, calling Tibby. He felt sure she must have been caught in a trap.

"Tibby, Tibby, Tibby!" he cried. "Where are you? Tibby, Tibby, Tibby!"

For some time he could hear nothing but the wind in the trees and the singing of the birds. Then he thought he heard a small mew.

"Tibby!" he shouted. "Tibby!"

"Miaow!" said a pussy-voice, and up ran Tibby to Jimmy, and purred and rubbed herself against his legs.

"Oh, dear Tibby!" said Jimmy, really delighted to see his cat again. He picked her up in his arms and made a fuss of her. She purred loudly, and then tried to get down.

"No, I'll carry you home, Tibby," said Jimmy, and he turned to go home. But Tibby struggled very hard, and at last he had to let her go. She ran into the woods and disappeared. Jimmy was very much puzzled. He went after her.

"Tibby! Why don't you want to come home with me?" he called. "Come back! Where are you going?"

Tibby mewed from somewhere; then Jimmy saw her bright green eyes looking at him from a nearby bush! He ran up and knelt down to see where she was.

And will you believe it, Tibby was lying comfortably down in the fine new basket that Jimmy had lost when he was looking for the bird's nest! There she was, as cosy as anything, looking up at Jimmy.

She was just as astonished as he was! "Oh, Tibby, what darling little kittens!" she cried. "You shall have them in your own cosy basket by the fire! Fancy you finding our basket in the woods and putting your kittens there!"

"Mummy, I needn't spend my money on a new basket now, need I?" said Jimmy, pleased. "I can buy my tunnel with my money."

"Of course!" said his mother. "We will just put Tibby comfortably in her own basket with the kittens, and then we will catch the bus and go and buy your tunnel. You deserve it, really, Jimmy, because you gave up your afternoon's play with Billy to go and hunt for Tibby—and you found a basket of surprises, didn't you?"

So everyone was happy, and Jimmy got his railway tunnel after all. As for Tibby, she was very happy to be made such a fuss of, and you should have seen her kittens when they grew! They were the prettiest, dearest little things you could wish to see. I know, because, you see, I've got one of them for my own!

But there was still another surprise for the little boy, for when Tibby jumped out of the basket, what do you suppose he saw at the bottom? Why, five beautiful little tabby kittens, all exactly like Tibby! He stared and stared and stared! He simply couldn't believe his eyes!

"Oh, Tibby!" he said. "Oh, Tibby! I've found you—and the basket—and some kittens, too! Oh, whatever will Mummy say!"

He picked up the basket with the kittens and set off home. Tibby ran beside him mewing. When he got home he called his mother and showed her his surprising find.

"Do Pass It On"

There was once a boy who liked doing kind things, and whenever people said to him—"It *is* kind of you to help me. Now what can I do for you in return?"—what do you think he said to them?

He said, "Oh, do pass it on! I don't want anything in return—just pass my bit of kindness on to somebody else. That's what my mother says we should do if people are good to us—pass it on!"

Well, that was a funny thing to say, but it was a very good idea. And now, just listen to what happened to a bit of kindness that was passed on!

Harry, the boy who began the bit of kindness, helped the old apple-woman to pick up the apples that fell out of her basket one morning. The old dame tripped over the kerb and down she went, with her apples all over the road! Dear, dear! She was so upset!

But along came Harry, helped her up, picked up all the apples, polished them with a clean handkerchief, and set them neatly back into the basket.

"You're a kind lad!" said the old apple-woman. "What can I do to repay you for your kindness? Will you have an apple?"

"No thank you," said Harry. "Just pass my bit of kindness on, will you?"

And off he went. "Very well!" thought the apple-woman. "I'll pass that bit of kindness on. I'll just wait and see how I can do it."

So down the road she went with her load, and very soon she came to where a woman was hanging out clothes on her line. Just as the apple-woman went by, the wind took hold of a pillow-case and blew it over the hedge. It was almost in the mud. The apple-woman ran to it, and caught it before it got dirty. The washer-woman was so grateful.

38

"That's kind of you," she said. "Very kind indeed."

"Do pass it on then!" said the apple-woman, pleased. "You pass on that bit of kindness, and don't forget!"

So the washer-woman thought about it and watched for a chance to pass it on. And very soon her chance came.

A little girl came down the road, crying. The washer-woman called out to her: "What's the matter, little girl?"

"Oh, I've been home, but my mother's out and I can't get any tea," wept the little girl. "And I'm so hungry!"

"Poor child!" said the washer-woman. "Come along in, and I'll give you some bread and treacle. I've got a bit of kindness to pass on to-day!"

So the child sat down and ate a great piece of bread and treacle. "You are very kind," she said shyly. "I wish I could give you back some bread and treacle."

"I don't want it, child," said the washer-woman. "Just pass the bit of kindness on—now don't forget. Do pass it on!"

The little girl ran off, pleased. She thought it was a funny idea to pass a bit of kindness on, but she made up her mind that she would. Her chance soon came. She passed the cottage where Mrs. Kelly lived with all her children, and saw poor Mrs. Kelly at the door, looking very worried.

"What's the matter?" asked the little girl.

"Oh, I heard my Johnny's fallen down in the next street, and his leg's hurt so much he can't walk home," said Mrs. Kelly. "I want to go and fetch him, but I daren't leave the other children alone in the house—they're so little!"

"Well, I've got a bit of kindness to pass on," said the little girl. "I'll mind them for you, Mrs. Kelly!"

So Mrs. Kelly ran off to fetch Johnny, and the little girl minded the children and played with them. When Mrs. Kelly came back with Johnny, she was very grateful.

"I'd give you a penny for your kindness but I haven't one to spare," she said.

"Oh, I don't want any payment," said the little girl. "But, Mrs. Kelly, do pass it on!"

"Pass what on?" said Mrs. Kelly in great surprise.

39

"My bit of kindness!" said the little girl, laughing, and she ran home.

Well, Mrs. Kelly thought she certainly *would* pass it on, and she kept her eyes open to see how she could do it. She didn't have to wait very long.

When she passed the park gates with her children, she saw the park-keeper looking very miserable indeed.

"What's the matter, park-keeper?" she said. "Is your wife ill, or something?"

"Oh no," said the man. "But I forgot to bring my tea with me this afternoon, and I'm cold. I wish I had a drop of hot tea to warm me up!"

"Oh, I'll send my Bobby to fetch it for you," said Mrs. Kelly at once. "He knows where your house is."

"Thanks very much," said the park-keeper. "It's very, very kind of you. Anything I can do for you, by any chance?"

"No," said Mrs. Kelly. "Just pass it on, that's all!"

The park-keeper laughed. He promised he would, but he couldn't seem to think what to do. When six o'clock came, he rang the bell for everyone to go out of the park, and soon it was empty. He locked the gate behind him, and went on his way home, down by the park railings.

And just by the railings he saw a little boy looking upset. It was Harry, the one who began this story of passing on.

"What's up, Harry?" asked the keeper.

"My best ball's gone over the railings," said Harry. "I'm so afraid someone else will find it in the morning. Then I shan't have it any more."

The keeper remembered the bit of kindness he had to pass on. "I'll go back to the park gates and unlock them for you," he said. "Then you can slip in and get your ball. What about that?"

"Oh, I say, that is nice of you!" said Harry, delighted. "But aren't you on your way home?"

"Oh, that doesn't matter," said the keeper. "I have got a bit of kindness to pass on, so perhaps this will do!" And back he went and unlocked the gates for Harry.

Harry got his ball and thanked the keeper. "Now just you pass that bit of kindness on!" said the keeper, smiling.

Well, wasn't it queer how Harry's own bit of kindness came back to him? He's busy passing it on again—and it may come to you this time. Do pass it on, won't you!

Visitors in the Night

The toys were very tired. They had had a very exciting day because the children had friends to tea—and all the toys had been played with.

"I simply can't keep my eyes open," said the pink cat. "It's no use. I must go to sleep."

"So must I," said the curly-haired doll. "I've been undressed and dressed so often today that I feel quite worn-out. I shall get into my cot and go to sleep."

And so, when somebody came into the playroom in the middle of the night, nobody was awake! The bear was giving tiny little snores in his corner, and the pink cat was all curled up in hers.

Somebody pattered in from a hole behind the cupboard, and squeaked loudly: "A message! I bring a message!"

Nobody answered. Nobody saw the small brown mouse with the twitching nose and long whiskers. He stood there in the middle of the floor, looking round in surprise.

"Isn't anyone awake? I bring a message. A MOST important message."

Still nobody woke up. The mouse looked for his best friend there—Clicky, the clockwork mouse. Ah, there he was. He ran over to him and pulled his tail hard.

"Clicky! Wake up! I've got a MESSAGE!"

Clicky woke up with a jump. "Dear me! What are you pulling my tail like that for?" he squealed.

"I've got a message from the five little fairies who live in Bluebell Wood," said the mouse, excitedly. "They came to a party given by the pixie who lives in our own garden and, oh dear, they've fallen in the pond!"

"Goodness!" said the clockwork mouse. "Are they wet?"

"Yes, they're soaked through," said the real mouse. "And they sent me here with a message. Can the dolls' house dolls let them sleep in the dolls' house tonight? They simply *must* dry themselves, and get to bed, else they will have dreadful colds."

"I'll wake the little dolls," said Clicky at once and soon he was knocking at the dolls' house door *rat-a-tat-a-tat*! The little mother-doll answered the door in her night-dress, most surprised.

When she heard about the wet fairies, she was quite upset. "The poor things! Mouse, go and bring them here at once. Are they small enough to come up your hole? They are? That's good. Then they will be small enough to sleep in the beds in my little dolls' house."

Off went the mouse at once, and the dolls' house dolls began to be very busy indeed. They ran water in the little bath —they put out clean towels—they made the beds and warmed blankets by the tiny kitchen fire. What excitement there was!

Soon five wet, miserable little fairies came trooping out of the mouse-hole with the mouse leading them. All the toys welcomed them, because Clicky had told them the news, of course. They were all awake now, and anxious to make the tiny fairies happy.

"It's so kind of you," said Tippitty, the biggest fairy. "We're so wet and cold!"

The mother-doll welcomed them into the dolls' house at once. "A hot bath for you!" she said. "And warm beds. And we'll give you hot soup to drink when you're in bed. I'll dry your clothes while you're asleep."

The five fairies felt much better after a nice hot bath. They wiped themselves dry with the little towels, and then put on nighties belonging to the dolls' house dolls. They fitted them beautifully.

"Into bed with you," said the kind little mother-doll. "Now—here comes your soup!"

Soon the five fairies were drinking hot soup out of the tea-set cups. They felt warm and happy. How lucky they were to find a little house like this, with beds just the right size.

"We shan't get colds now," said Tippitty. "We shall feel quite all right in the morning. Oh, what a comfortable bed this is!"

Soon all five had snuggled down. The mother-doll tucked them up. "Please will you leave the light on?" asked Tippitty. "Just in case we wake up and have forgotten where we are!"

So the lights were left on in the little house—and the toys came creeping to the windows to peep in.

"Look—there they are, tucked up in the little dolls' beds," whispered the golliwog. "Aren't they sweet?"

"They are just the right size," said the pink cat. "Aren't we lucky to have five fairies sleeping here tonight? It is a very great honour."

They crept back to the toy cupboard and fell asleep again. The dolls' house dolls went to sleep too. Everyone was really very tired.

They didn't wake up till quite late. One of the children came scampering in at eight o'clock, on her way down to breakfast. She stopped in surprise when she saw the dolls' house.

"Why! The lights are on!" she cried. "Jane! Come and see! Somebody has left the dolls' house lights on!"

Jane came running in too. "Goodness, Eileen—who could have left them on?" she said. "I know we turned them off last night. Let's look inside and see if anything has gone wrong with them."

Good gracious me! What a to-do there was in the dolls' house when the dolls heard the children outside! The mother-doll woke up the five fairies at once.

"Quick! You must dress and go," she said. "The children are here—they may catch you and take you to school to show their friends!"

But there wasn't time to dress—Jane and Eileen were looking through the windows—and they saw the five fairies hopping out of bed in a hurry.

They stared as if they couldn't believe their eyes. Then they ran to their mother's room. "Mummy! Mummy, do come! There are fairies in our doll's house! Come quickly. They're the prettiest things you ever saw!"

But when their mother came to the playroom and went to look in at the windows, there were no fairies to be seen!

They had caught up their clothes, fled down the little dolls' house stairs, run across the floor, and disappeared down the mousehole at top speed. Tippitty fell over her night-dress, but picked herself up just in time.

"Oh! There's nobody here now!" said Jane, in dismay.

"There never was," said Mummy, laughing. "It was just a joke of yours."

"It wasn't!" said Eileen. "And look—the front door is open now—and see, one of the fairies has dropped a little petticoat as she ran! Oh, what a pretty, cobwebby thing!"

She showed her mother the tiny petticoat. Tippitty had dropped it without knowing.

"Well—it's a most extraordinary thing—and I don't really believe it!" said Mummy. "Now, do come and have your breakfast. Bring the tiny petticoat to show Daddy, if you like—but he won't believe your tale either."

He didn't, of course—but he would have if he had peeped in at the playroom the next night, and had seen five small fairies tripping out of the mousehole with parcels under their arms—the night-dresses belonging to the dolls' house dolls, all beautifully washed and ironed!

"Thank you for your help last night," said Tippitty. "And here are the night-dresses you lent us—and also a little magic spell in a box. It will grant you any wish you like—but only one—so think carefully before you use it!"

Well, what a surprise—a magic wish of their own! They simply can't wait to use it—and I really do wonder what they will wish for, don't you?

Smack-Biff-Thud!

Mister Flick lived next door to Dame Tantrum. Flick was hot-tempered and Dame Tantrum was always flying into a rage, so very often there were shouts and yells coming from their gardens.

But for a long time there had been peace. Mister Flick was growing cucumbers in a frame to show at the Fruit and Flower Show in the village, and he was afraid of quarrelling with Dame Tantrum in case she threw rubbish into his garden and broke his frames.

Dame Tantrum was growing tomatoes out of doors, also for the Show, and she didn't want Mister Flick throwing rubbish into *her* garden either, in case it broke her beautiful tomato plants.

"Ha!" said Mister Flick to himself each morning, as he went to look at his long green cucumbers. "Ha! I'm quite sure there are no finer cucumbers in the village! I shall walk off with first prize, that's certain!"

And Dame Tantrum would look lovingly at her fat tomatoes getting red and round, and rub her hands together in delight. "Best tomatoes in the kingdom!" she said to herself. "And all grown in the open air too! I shall get first prize, there's no doubt of it!"

The great Fruit and Flower Show drew nearer. Mister Flick and Dame Tantrum grew excited. They looked at their cucumbers and tomatoes a dozen times a day. Mister Flick gave his cucumbers four canfuls of water each evening. Dame Tantrum gave her tomatoes a canful for each plant. And the green cucumbers and red tomatoes grew and grew and grew.

Now one evening Mister Flick cut a cucumber for his own supper. The same evening Dame Tantrum picked three ripe tomatoes for *her* supper, and they happened to see one another just going up the garden.

"Good evening," said Mister Flick. "Look at this cucumber. Did you ever see such a fine monster?"

"Good evening," said Dame Tantrum. "Look at my tomatoes! I'm sure you have never grown such beauties."

"I don't care for tomatoes," said Mister Flick. "Nasty soft things. Give me a cucumber any time!"

"I've never been able to understand what people see in cucumbers," said Dame Tantrum, offended. "No sweetness, all water and tough flesh!"

"Don't talk nonsense," said Mister Flick.

He held up his fine long curved cucumber and waggled it in front of Dame Tantrum's face. "Look at that for a fine cucumber!"

"Stop waggling the ugly thing under my nose!" cried Dame Tantrum, losing her temper. "It's a silly cucumber. Cucumbers sound silly and they look silly too!"

Mister Flick was angry. He shook the cucumber hard at Dame Tantrum, and, do you know, he shook it so hard that the top end flew off and hit Dame Tantrum on the nose!

Mister Flick was just as surprised as Dame Tantrum. When the old dame had got over her shock she screamed at Mister Flick. "You bad man! Throwing cucumbers at me! Well, I can do some throwing too. Take that!"

And she picked a nice ripe tomato out of her basket and threw it straight at Mister Flick. It hit him in the face, splosh!

"Ooooh!" said Mister Flick, astonished. "Now, Dame Tantrum, stop this! I won't have tomatoes thrown at me!"

"Oh, won't you! Well, have another!" said the cross dame, and she threw a second one at Mister Flick. He tried to dodge it and couldn't, and he fell back into one of his cucumber frames! By good luck the lid was off, so he didn't break any glass, but he sat down heavily on a fine cucumber plant!

"Oh, oh, my beautiful cucumbers!" cried Mister Flick, looking at three that he had broken in half. "Oh, you bad-tempered old dame! Take my broken cucumbers!"

And Mister Flick began to throw the broken halves of his cucumbers over the wall at Dame Tantrum! Well, really! That was more than she could stand!

"I'm as good a shot as you!" she cried, and she threw her third tomato at Mister

Flick. Plonk! It hit his forehead and the red juice dripped down Mister Flick's face. He quite lost his temper then.

"I'll teach you, I'll teach you!" he yelled, and he pulled at all the cucumbers he could see, waggled them hard at Dame Flick, and off flew the tops and hit her on the nose! Some people passing by stopped to gaze in surprise, and how they laughed!

Well, Dame Tantrum rushed at her tomato plants and pulled as many tomatoes as she could see. Soon she was pelting Mister Flick with them as if they were snowballs. Splash—thud—smack! And plop—biff! went the cucumbers! It was a sight to see!

tempers, you deserve to lose your prize vegetables. Clear up the mess, please."

They spent the evening clearing up the mess. It was dreadful to have to throw the cucumbers and tomatoes on the rubbish heap. Mister Flick saw Dame Tantrum crying, and he felt sorry for her.

He poked his head over the wall. "I'm sorry about it all," he said. "Let's be friends. It's too late now to grow cucumbers and tomatoes for the Show this week, but we'll have supper together one night with a salad of young cucumbers and tomatoes!"

So they did—and now they are great friends. They mean to take the first prizes next year, whatever happens.

Then Mister Plod the village policeman came by, and he was shocked. He went in at Dame Tantrum's garden gate and spoke sternly to the two sillies.

"Stop this at once!" he said. "Whatever do you think you are doing? I thought you were growing these lovely cucumbers and tomatoes for the Show!"

Mister Flick and Dame Tantrum stopped their throwing and stared at Mister Plod. Dame Tantrum suddenly saw her dozens of beautiful tomatoes smashed on the ground, and Mister Flick saw his fine cucumbers all in bits!

"Oh, I shan't win any prize now!" they both wailed. And Dame Tantrum burst into tears, and Mister Flick went as red as one of the tomatoes!

"It serves you right," said Mister Plod sternly. "If you can't manage your

Thirteen O'clock

Once upon a time Sandy was walking home from school when he saw an extra fine dandelion clock.

"What a beauty!" he said, picking it with its stalk. "I wonder if it will tell me the right time."

He blew it—puff! A cloud of fluffy white seeds flew away. There were plenty left on the clock. He blew again—puff! More fluff flew away on the breeze. Puff! Puff! Puff! He counted as he blew.

"One o'clock! Two o'clock! Three! Four! Five! Six o'clock! Seven! Eight! Nine! Ten! Eleven o'clock! Twelve o'clock! *Thirteen o'clock*!"

At the thirteenth puff there was no fluff left on the dandelion clock at all. It was just an empty stalk.

And then things began to happen.

A noise of little voices was heard, and Sandy looked down at his feet. Round him was a crowd of pixies, shouting loudly.

"Did you say thirteen o'clock? Hi, did you say thirteen o'clock?"

"Yes," said Sandy, in astonishment. "The dandelion clock said thirteen o'clock."

"Oh my goodness me, thirteen o'clock only happens once in a blue moon!" cried the biggest pixie. "Whatever shall we do?"

"Why, what's the matter?" asked Sandy. "What are you so upset about?"

"Don't you know?" shouted all the pixies together. "Why, at thirteen o'clock all the witches from Witchland fly on broomsticks, and if they see any elf, pixie, brownie or gnome out of Fairyland they catch them and take them away. Oh dear, goodness gracious, whatever shall we do?"

Sandy felt quite alarmed.

"Do they take little boys, too?" he asked.

"We don't know, but they might," answered the biggest pixie. "Hark! Can you hear the Witches' Wind blowing?"

Sandy listened. Yes, a wind was blowing up, and it sounded a funny sort of wind, all whispery and strange.

"That's the wind the witches use to blow their broomsticks along," said the pixies. "Little boy, you'd better run home quickly."

But Sandy wasn't going to leave the little pixies alone. They were frightened, so he felt he really must stay and look after them.

"I'll stay with you," he said. "But do you think you could make me as small as you, because if I'm as big as this the witches will see me easily and catch me."

"That's easy to do," said the biggest

pixie. "Shut your eyes, put your hands over your ears and whisper 'Hoona-looki-allo-pie' three times to yourself. Then you'll be as small as we are. When you want to get big again do exactly the same, but say the magic words backwards."

Sandy felt excited. He shut his eyes and covered his ears with his hands. Then he whispered the magic words three times—and lo and behold, when he opened his eyes again he was as small as the pixies! They crowded round him, laughing and talking.

"I am Gobbo," said the biggest one, "and this is my friend, Twinkle."

Sandy solemnly shook hands with Gobbo and Twinkle. Then, as the wind grew louder, the pixies crowded together in alarm, and looked up at the sky.

"Where shall we go to hide?" said Twinkle. "Oh, quick, think of somewhere, somebody, or the witches will be along and will take us prisoners!"

Everybody thought hard, and then Sandy had a good idea.

"As I came along I noticed an old saucepan thrown away in the hedge," he said. "Let's go and find it and get under it. It will hide us all beautifully."

Off went all the pixies, following Sandy. He soon found the saucepan, and by pushing hard they managed to turn it upside-down over them, so that it quite hid them. There was a hole in the side out of which they could peep.

"I've dropped my handkerchief," suddenly cried Twinkle, pointing to where a little red hanky lay on the ground some way off. "I must go and get it."

"No, don't," said Gobbo. "You'll be caught. The witches will be along any minute now. Hark how the wind is blowing!"

"But I must get it!" cried Twinkle. "If I don't the witches will catch sight of it out there, and down they'll all come to see what it is. Then they'll sniff pixies nearby and come hunting under this saucepan for us."

"Oooooooooh!" groaned all the pixies, in fright.

"Well, go and get it quickly!" said Gobbo to Twinkle. "Hurry up!"

Twinkle crept out from under the saucepan and everybody watched him anxiously. The wind grew louder and louder and all the tall grasses swayed like trees in the wind. Then there came a sort of voice in the wind and Sandy listened to hear what it said.

"The witches are coming, the witches are coming!" it said, in a deep-down, grumbling sort of voice, rushing into every hole and corner. Sandy peeped through the hole in the saucepan to see what Twinkle was doing. He was dodging here and there between the grasses. At last he reached the place where his red handkerchief lay, and he picked it up and put it into his pocket.

And then, oh my goodness, the pixies in the saucepan saw the first witches coming! They shouted to Twinkle, and he looked up in the sky. There they were, three witches in pointed hats and long cloaks, sitting on long broomsticks, flying through the cloudy sky.

"Quick, Twinkle, quick!" yelled Sandy and the pixies. How they hoped the witches wouldn't see him! He crouched down under a yellow buttercup till they were past, and then began to run to the saucepan.

"There's two more witches coming!" shouted the pixies, pointing. Sure enough, two more could be seen in the windy sky, much lower down than the others. Twinkle crept under a green stinging-nettle and stayed there without a movement till the witches had gone safely by.

"Poor Twinkle! He *will* be stung!" said Gobbo, sadly. When the two witches were past Twinkle ran from beneath the nettle straight to the saucepan and crept underneath in safety. How glad all the pixies were! They crowded round him and stroked his nettle-stung hands and face.

"Never mind, Twinkle, you're safe here," they said.

"Look at all the witches now!" cried Sandy peeping through the hole. "Oh my! What a wonderful sight! I'm glad I'm seeing this."

It certainly was a marvellous sight! The sky was simply full of flying witches, and some of them had black cats sitting behind them on the broomsticks. The cats coiled their tails round the sticks and held on like monkeys. It was funny to see them.

"Does this always happen at thirteen o'clock?" asked Sandy.

"Always," said Twinkle, solemnly. "But thirteen o'clock only happens once in a blue moon, as I told you before. The moon must have been blue this month. Did you notice it?"

"Well, no, I didn't," said Sandy. "I'm nearly always in bed when it's moonlight. Oh, I say! Look! One of the witches has lost her black cat!"

The pixies peeped out of the hole in the saucepan. Sure enough, one of the black cats had tumbled off its broomstick. It had tried to be clever and wash itself on the broomstick, and had lost its hold and tumbled off. It was falling through the air, and the witch was darting down with her broomstick, trying her best to catch it.

She just managed to grab hold of the cat

before it fell on the ground—but her broomstick was smashed to pieces, and the witch rolled over and over on the grass, holding the cat safely in her arms. She sat up and looked round. When she saw her broken broomstick she began to howl.

"It's broken. It's broken! I'll never be able to fly back home! Boo hoo hoo!"

Sandy was frightened to see the witch rolling over and over. He thought she would be sure to hurt herself. He was a very kind-hearted boy, and he longed to go and ask her if she was all right. He began to squeeze himself under the saucepan, meaning to go and see if the witch was hurt.

But the pixies tried to pull him back.

"Don't go, don't go," they whispered, for the witch was quite near. "She'll change you into a black-beetle."

"Why should she?" asked Sandy. "I'm going to be kind to her. Besides, she's got a nice face, rather like my grannie's—I'm sure she isn't a bad witch."

He wriggled himself away from the hands of the pixies and ran over to the witch. She was sitting down on the grass crying big tears all down her cheeks. The cat was on her lap, still looking frightened.

The witch was most surprised to see him. Sandy stopped just by her. She had a very tall pointed hat, and a long cloak round her shoulders, with silver suns, moons and stars all over it. The cat arched its back and spat angrily at the little boy.

"Excuse me," said Sandy, politely. "I saw you roll over on the ground when your broomstick broke, and I came to see if you were hurt."

"Well," said the witch, holding out her left hand, "I'm not much hurt—but my hand is a bit cut. I must have hit it against a stone when I rolled over."

"I'll tie it up for you with my hand-kerchief," said Sandy. "It's quite clean."

The witch looked more astonished than ever. She held out her hand and Sandy tied it up very neatly.

"Thank you," said the witch. "That's most kind of you. Oh dear—just look at my poor broomstick—it's broken in half! I shall never get back to Witchland again!"

Sandy looked at the broomstick. The broom part was all right, but the stick was broken. Sandy felt in his pocket to see if he had brought his knife with him. Yes, he had!

"I'll cut you another stick from the hedge," he said. "Then you can fit it into the broomhead and use it to fly away with!"

"You're the cleverest, kindest boy I ever met!" said the witch. "Thank you so much! Most people are afraid of witches, you know, because they think we will change them into black-beetles, or something— but that's an old-fashioned idea. The old witches *were* like that—but nowadays we witches are decent folk, making magic spells that will do no one any harm at all."

"Well, I'm glad to hear *that*!" said Sandy, hoping that the pixies under the saucepan were hearing it, too. He went to the hedge and cut another stick for the witch. He fitted it neatly into the broomhead and threw away the broken stick. The witch was very pleased.

She said a magic spell over it to make it able to fly. Then she turned to Sandy.

"Won't you have a ride with me?" she asked. "It is great fun. I will see that you are safe."

"Ooh, I'd *love* a ride!" cried Sandy, in delight. "But you are sure you won't take me away to Witchland?"

"I told you that witches don't do horrid things now," said the witch. "Do I *look* like a nasty witch?"

"No, you don't," said Sandy. "Well, I'll come for a ride—I'd love to! I'll be awfully late for my dinner but an adventure like this doesn't come often!"

He perched himself on the broomstick, behind the witch, who took her black cat on her knee. Just as they were about to set off, there came a great clatter, and the saucepan nearby was overturned by the pixies. They streamed out, shouting and calling.

"Take us for a ride, too! Take us for a ride, too!"

The witch looked at them in amazement. She had had no idea that any pixies were near. She laughed when she saw where they had been hiding.

"Climb up on the stick," she said. "I'll give you a ride, too!"

Goodness, there wasn't room to put a blade of grass on that broomstick after all the pixies had climbed up on it! What a squash there was, to be sure!

The witch called out a string of magic words and the broomstick suddenly flew up into the air with a jerk. Sandy held on tightly. The pixies yelled in delight and began to sing joyfully. All the other witches flying by in the sky laughed to see such a crowded broomstick. Sandy did enjoy himself. He was very high up, and the wind whistled in his ears and blew his hair straight back from his head.

"Now we're going down again!" said the witch, and the broomstick swooped downwards. It landed gently and all the pixies tumbled off in a heap. Sandy jumped off and thanked the witch very much for such a lovely ride.

"I must go now," she said. "The hour of thirteen o'clock is nearly over and I must return to Witchland. Good-bye, kind little boy, and I'll give you another ride next time it's thirteen o'clock. If you wait for me here, I'll take you all the way to Witchland and back!"

Off she went, she and her black cat, and left Sandy standing in the grass, watching her fly away. The pixies waved to the witch and she waved back.

"Well, that *was* an adventure!" cried the pixies. "We'll never be afraid of witches again, that's certain! Hurray!"

"I wonder what the time is," said Sandy. "What comes after thirteen o'clock? Is it fourteen o'clock?"

"Oh no!" said Twinkle. "Thirteen o'clock just comes and goes. It isn't any time really. It always comes after twelve o'clock, but it's followed by one o'clock as if nothing had happened in between!"

Somewhere a church clock chimed the hour. Sandy listened. Then the clock struck one, and no more.

"One o'clock, one o'clock!" cried the pixies their voices growing small and faint. "Thirteen o'clock is over! Good-bye, good-bye!"

Sandy looked at them—they were vanishing like the mist, and in a moment or two he could see nothing of them. They just weren't there.

"I must make myself big again," he thought. He remembered the words quite well. He shut his eyes and covered up his ears. He had to say the magic words backwards, so he thought hard before he spoke.

55

"Pie-allo-looki-hoona!" he said. When he opened his eyes he was his own size again! He set off home, running as fast as he could, for he was afraid that his mother would be wondering where he was.

He ran into the house and found his mother just putting out his dinner. She didn't seem to think he was late at all!

"You're just in nice time," she said to Sandy. "Good boy! You must have come straight from school without stopping!"

"But mother—ever such a lot has happened since I left school," said Sandy, in surprise. "I'm dreadfully late!"

"No, darling, it's only just gone one o'clock," said his mother, looking at the clock.

"Didn't *you* have thirteen o'clock too, this morning?" asked Sandy, sitting down to his dinner.

"What *are* you talking about?" said his mother with a laugh. "Thirteen o'clock! Whoever heard of that? That only happens in Fairyland, once in a blue moon, I should think!"

Sandy thought about it. Perhaps it was true—perhaps thirteen o'clock belonged to the fairies, and not to the world of boys and girls. How lucky he had been to have that one magic hour of thirteen o'clock with the pixies and the witch. And next time it was thirteen o'clock he was going to ride on a broomstick again. Oh, what fun!

"I do hope it will be thirteen o'clock again soon," he said.

"Eat up your dinner and don't talk nonsense!" said his mother, laughing.

But it wasn't nonsense, was it? Sandy is going to blow all the dandelion clocks he sees so that he will know when it is thirteen o'clock again. If you blow them too, you may find that magic hour as well!

The Adventurous Ball

There was once a big round ball. It was all colours—red, yellow, blue, and green, and it looked very gay indeed when it bounced or rolled.

The other toys were rather impatient with the ball. They thought it a silly, dull creature. It could do nothing but bounce.

"What a life you lead!' said the sailing boat to the ball. "Nothing but bounce, bounce, bounce! Look at me! I go sailing on the river and on the pond. I even go on the sea at seaside time!"

"And what about *me*?" said the toy bus. "When I'm wound up I go round and round the nursery, and I carry dolls, bears, and rabbits for passengers! I have a fine life!"

"And I fly up in the air and see all kinds of things!" said the toy aeroplane.

"So do I!" said the kite. "I fly above the clouds and see the birds up there, and get as near to the sun as I can get!"

"And we dolls get about a lot too," said the curly-haired doll. We go out in prams—we are taken out to tea—we do see the world! Poor, dull ball, you do nothing but bounce. We are sorry for you."

The ball felt sorry for himself, too. He had never felt dull before the toys had said all this to him, but now he really did feel as if he led a miserable sort of life.

However, the time came when all that was changed, as you will hear. It happened that the children in whose nursery the toys lived went off to the seaside for a holiday,

and with them they took most of their toys. The bus went, the dolls went, the aeroplane, the kite—and the ball. What fun!

And then the ball's adventures began. It had longed and longed for adventures, and it was surprised when it had some. It had been taken down to the beach and left on the sand whilst the children dug castles. Nobody noticed that the tide was coming up. No one noticed that the tide had reached the ball. And no one saw that it had taken away the ball when it began to go out again!

But it had! It bobbed the ball up and down on little waves, and took it right out to sea!

"Good gracious!" said the ball to itself. "I might be a little boat, the way I am floating along! Wherever am I going?"

A fish popped up its head and spoke to the ball. "Hallo, big round fellow! What news of the land have you?"

The ball was proud to be able to tell news. It told the fish all about the other toys. Then the fish told the ball about the sea, and all the fishes and other sea-creatures in it. "You are a bold, brave ball to go adventuring off by yourself like this," said the fish. "I do admire you!"

The ball bobbed on, prouder than ever. Soon a big white sea-gull swooped down and came to rest just by the ball. "Hallo, big round fellow," he said in surprise. "I thought you might be food. How very bold of you to come adventuring on the sea like this!'

The ball felt proud—but it was a truthful ball. "Well, as a matter of fact, I can't very well help this adventure," he said. "The sea took me away."

"Tell me news of the land," said the gull. So the ball told all about the other toys, and the gull then told him of the gulls, and of their seaweed nests, and young brown gull-babies. He told the ball of stormy days at sea. He showed him how he dived for fish. The ball was pleased and excited. How nice everyone was to him!

The ball bobbed in the pool and listened to the tales the crabs and shrimps told him. He heard about the children who came shrimping with a big net. He saw how the little crabs could bury themselves in the sand in two twinks and not show even a leg. It was all very wonderful to the big ball.

When the tide went out again the ball went with it. It bobbed along merrily. Suddenly it saw a great big thing coming straight at it. Oh dear, oh dear—it was an enormous steamer! The ball felt sure it would be squashed to bits—but at the last moment it bobbed to one side and the big steamer sailed on. "Look! Look!" cried the people on the steamer, leaning over the side.

"There is a fine big ball, bobbing along all by itself!"

The ball was proud to be noticed by the people on the steamer. It bobbed after it for a long way but then got left behind. The tide took it once more and some great big waves curled over it and almost buried it. But it bobbed up gaily again, wondering what adventure it would have next.

As it floated along it saw a little boat with two children in. "Look! Look! There's a beautiful big ball!" cried the boy. "Let's get it!"

The ball floated on. The tide turned again and flowed into a big bay. The ball floated by a boat and stayed there for a while. The boat spoke to him and told him how he sometimes went out fishing and how little boys and girls went rowing in him and used him for bathing. The ball had never known such a lot of things in his life. He would have stayed by the boat for a longer time, but a little wave came and took him away. He floated into a rock-pool, and there the crabs and shrimps swam up to him in admiration.

"What a fine big round fellow you are!" they said. "Where do you come from? How brave of you to adventure all alone on the big, big sea!"

The boat was rowed after the ball. The boy leaned out and took it. He shook the water from it and showed it to his sister.

"Do you know, Winnie, I believe it is our very own ball—the one we lost yesterday!" said the boy. "See the colours on it! I am quite sure it is our own ball!"

"So it is!" said the girl. "I wonder where it has been all this time! I wish it could tell us its adventures. I expect it has had such a lot, bobbing up and down on the sea."

The children took the ball back to shore. There were all the other toys—the aeroplane, the bus, the dolls, the kite, and all the rest. How surprised they were to see the ball again!

"We saw you floating away!" cried the aeroplane. "Where did you go?"

"Ah," said the ball proudly. "I'm a big round adventurous fellow, I am! I've talked with birds and fishes, crabs and shrimps—I've heard tales from boats—I've nearly been run down by a great steamer, and all the people on it saw me! You may think I'm a dull fellow and can do nothing but bounce—but you are mistaken—I can float too—and I've had more adventures than the whole lot of you put together!"

And after that, as you can imagine, none of the toys ever laughed at the ball again for being a dull fellow who could do nothing but bounce! He could tell more stories than any one else—and he says he is going to float away again next year and have some more adventures. I wonder if he will!

When Mrs. Tumpy lost her head

Mrs. Tumpy lived in Peppermint Village in a little cottage called Toffee Roofs. She was a fat, round goblin woman, and all the elves, pixies and goblins in the village used to laugh at her because she fussed so much.

If one of her hens got loose she would run for miles asking anyone if they had seen it—and maybe it was under her henhouse all the while!

If she cut her little finger she would cry and scream, and somebody else would have to bind it up for her because she was so upset. And, dear me, one day when the wind caught her open umbrella and took her galloping down the village street, squealing for help, everyone thought she was being chased by robbers or something.

They came running out of their houses in fright. "Why, it's only that the wind has caught her open umbrella, like a ship's sail, and sent her scudding along," said Jinky, in

disgust. "Hey, Mrs. Tumpy—leave go the handle and you'll be all right."

But Mrs. Tumpy was so scared that she quite lost her head. She wouldn't let go the umbrella handle, and the wind took her right to the duck-pond. She ran in at top speed and then sank. It took a long time to drag her out.

The cat had been there first. The jug was upset and the milk was on the floor. Mrs. Tumpy flew into a rage, and began to fuss round angrily.

"Oh dear, dear, dear! Now what shall I do? No milk, and there's Dame Quickly coming to tea. No time to get any more. Oh, where's that cat! Tabby, Tabby, Tabby!"

The cat came, but she didn't hear it. She turned to go to the stove and fell over it. Crash! She knocked her best teapot off the table.

"Oh, my, look at that! Nothing but bad luck today. Now what am I to do? Oh, goodness knows how I shall ever get the tea ready at this rate."

There was a voice outside the front door and Mrs. Tumpy heard the tap-tap-tap of Dame Quickly's stick as the old lady walked into the hall. "Now, now, Mrs. Tumpy, fussing again, and losing your head over something! Dear, dear. . . ."

Dame Quickly walked into the kitchen, and then she stopped in amazement, staring at Mrs. Tumpy.

"What's the matter?" said Mrs. Tumpy, crossly. "Haven't I done my hair?"

She turned to look at herself in the big

glass—and then she gave a scream of dismay.

"Where's my head? I've lost it! Oh, mercy me, what's happened to my head?"

"Oh, Mrs. Tumpy, we always said you'd lose it if you went on like that," said Dame Quickly, "and now you have."

"Oh, oh—what shall I do? Where's my head gone?" wept Mrs. Tumpy, and tears from where her head ought to be fell down the front of her dress. She looked all round the kitchen, but her head wasn't there. She even went and looked into the larder, but of course it was nowhere to be seen.

She ran out into the garden. "Has anyone seen my head?" she called to the astonished passers-by. "I've lost my head! Has anyone seen it?"

"Now, Mrs. Tumpy," said Jinky, when she was drying in front of his fire. "Listen to me. You fuss too much. You lose your

head at the smallest upset. You are always making people think that something dreadful is happening to you, and all the time it's only a spider that has come out of a corner and made you jump—or something like that."

"Don't talk to me like that," said Mrs. Tumpy, crossly. "I won't have it."

"Well, you take my advice," said Jinky. "Don't lose your head too often—or one day it really will pop off—and never come back!"

But Mrs. Tumpy took no notice of his words at all, and she still went on squealing at nothing, making terrible fusses, and calling for help if she even saw an earwig.

So Jinky grinned a little grin to himself, and made up his mind to give Mrs. Tumpy a shock. He went to his grandmother, Dame Know-a-Lot, and asked her for a disappearing spell. She gave him one in a box. It was a blue powder.

"Whatever it's blown on will disappear," said Dame Know-a-Lot. "It will still be there, of course, but no one will see it. Take care how you use it, Jinky."

Now that afternoon Jinky walked quietly by Mrs. Tumpy's garden. He peeped over the wall and saw what he had expected to see—Mrs. Tumpy fast asleep in a deck-chair.

Mrs. Tumpy soon woke up. She looked at her watch. Dear, dear, it was teatime already. And Dame Quickly was coming to tea! Up she got and ran indoors. Soon she had the kettle on and went to the larder for the milk.

Now most people guessed at once that someone had put a spell on Mrs. Tumpy to make her head invisible, and they laughed. But they weren't going to tell Mrs. Tumpy why. Oh, dear me, no! Perhaps if she thought she really *had* lost her head, she wouldn't make such silly fusses as she did.

So everyone shook their heads, and said the same thing. "No, Mrs. Tumpy—so sorry, but we haven't seen your head anywhere. Dear, dear, we always said you'd lose it if you went on kicking up such a fuss about everything."

Poor Mrs. Tumpy couldn't eat any tea, or any supper either. She spent all the evening looking in the most unlikely places for her lost head. She even looked in the coal-scuttle and under the bed.

She went to bed very unhappy indeed. "I can't clean my teeth or brush my hair because my head has gone," she groaned. And then she was so tired out that she fell asleep.

In the night the spell wore off. When she awoke and looked fearfully at herself in the glass, how excited she was to find that her head had come back again. She smiled and nodded at it.

"So you're back. Welcome home to me! I *am* glad to see you. And I do promise I'll never lose you again, dear head, never, never, never!"

And she was very careful after that not to lose her head or fuss when anything went wrong. So Jinky's mischievous little spell did some good after all.

Jinky smiled to himself. He jumped over the wall, and went on tiptoe to Mrs. Tumpy. He took out his box of blue powder and blew it gently over her head. Then he went back over the wall.

He stood and watched. Mrs. Tumpy's head gradually faded away and disappeared. How peculiar she looked! Jinky could still hear her snoring. He tiptoed away, smiling.

The Little Musical Box

In the playroom was a dear little musical box. It was quite round, and it had a handle that could be turned. When you turned the handle, the music played.

"Tiddley-iddley-oh-lee-oh," went the music, and the toys danced to it night after night.

"It's funny to think that music is shut up in this box, isn't it?" said the little doll in the blue dress. "I do like it."

The goldfish in the big glass bowl up on the window-sill tapped his nose against the glass. That meant that he wanted to speak to the toys. So the golliwog climbed up to listen.

"Bring the music up here," said the goldfish, in his bubbly voice. "I want to hear it too."

So the golly and the teddy carried the little round box carefully up to the goldfish bowl. The bear turned the handle and the music played merrily. "Tiddley-idd-ley, oh-lee-oh!"

"Oh, it's lovely!" said the goldfish and he waved his tail about in time to the music. "Please do sometimes bring it on the window-sill for me to hear."

The toys never played the music until it was night-time, and the three children were in bed. They loved Freda, Mollie and John, and were always excited when they came to play with them. But when they were in bed and asleep it would never do to make a noise and wake them up.

The golly always pushed the door almost shut when they played the musical box at night, or raced round the floor in the little clockwork engine. They really had fun then, especially if the engine-driver was in a good temper and let some of them drive the engine themselves.

One night, when the toys were playing together, there came a great wind that blew outside, and made the trees sway and bend.

"Listen to that!" said the bear. "What a noise!"

"I can hear the rain on the window now," said the little black doll. "Drip-drip-drip, drop-drop-drop!"

"And I can *feel* it!" said the golly, suddenly. "Goodness, where's my umbrella!"

"Don't be silly! The window is shut," said the bear.

"Well, it isn't—look, the wind has blown it open," said the black doll. "I can feel the rain coming in too. And just see how the curtains are blowing!"

The wind had blown so hard that the window had been jerked wide open! It was swinging to and fro, and the curtains were flapping wildly.

The goldfish in his bowl up on the window-sill was frightened. He tapped on the glass with his nose. "The curtain is flapping against my bowl!" he said, in his little bubbling voice. "I'm afraid!"

"Goodness! I hope the curtains don't overturn his bowl!" said the golliwog—and do you know, just as he said that, the wind blew the curtains so hard that they pushed the goldfish bowl right over!

Crash! It tipped on its side and all the water poured out of it in a rush, splashing down the wall to the floor below.

"The goldfish! He's been tipped out too!" cried the black doll. "Oh, Goldie! Are you hurt?"

The little fish was flapping about on the carpet, panting for breath. "I can't breathe when I'm out of the water!" he said. "Water! Put me in water! Quick!"

But there wasn't any water to put him in. There wasn't even a vase of flowers he could be slipped into! The toys were in a terrible worry about him.

"He can't breathe! Water, water!" cried the bear. But it wasn't a bit of good shouting out for water. The bathroom was a long way away and water didn't come by itself!

"We'll carry him to the bathroom!" said the doll in the blue dress. "Perhaps there is some water in the bath."

But, you know, the goldfish was so very slippery that nobody could hold him. He just slipped out of their hands, and flapped back on to the carpet again.

And then the golliwog had a wonderful idea. "Where's the musical box? Let's carry it into the children's bedroom and play it as fast as we can!"

"Oh yes—then they'll wake up and come and see what's happening!" cried the bear. "They'll see poor old Goldie!"

The golliwog and the bear took hold of the musical box and carried it out of the door, down the passage and in at the door of the children's bedroom. It felt very heavy to them, because they weren't very big.

They put it down on the bedroom floor with a bump. "Now!" said the bear, and he took hold of the handle. He turned it quickly and the music came tinkling out, loud and clear and sweet.

"Tiddley-iddley-oh-lee-oh! Tiddley-iddley-oh-lee-oh!" The musical box played its little tune on and on, and the golly and bear took turns at winding the handle round and round.

Freda woke up first. She sat up, surprised. "Why—it sounds like the musical box!" she said, and she woke up John and Mollie. They sat up and heard it too.

Mollie switched on her torch—and there, in its light, she saw the bear and the golly with the musical box, playing it without stopping!

"Look! Oh look! It's Teddy and Golly with our musical box!" cried Mollie. "Why have they brought it here?"

Just as she said that, Golly and Teddy lifted the musical box and hurried out of the room, hoping that the children would follow them to the playroom.

They did, of course—and the very first thing they saw was poor old Goldie flapping very feebly on the floor. He was in a very bad way now, and the children had only just come in time.

"Goldie! You're out of your bowl! Oh look—the wind blew the window open, and the curtains must have knocked over the bowl!" cried John.

Mollie took the bowl and ran to the bathroom.

She filled it with water and ran back. John picked up poor Goldie very gently and slid him into the bowl.

He flapped feebly and turned on his side. The children and the toys watched him, hardly daring to breathe. Would Goldie be all right?

He turned the right way up again. He moved his fins more strongly. His mouth opened and shut as he took in the water he had missed so much. He gasped a few words in his little bubbly voice.

"Thank you! I'll be all right now!"

"Well!" said Freda, in surprise, looking round at the toys, "WHO had the bright idea of waking us up with the musical box so that we could save poor Goldie? You are very good, clever toys—and tomorrow we will give a party for you, just to show you how grateful we are!"

They shut the window tightly so that the wet curtains hung still and straight. The bowl would not be knocked over again!

"Good-night," said the children, and went back to bed—and in the morning they wondered if they had dreamed it all!

"No—we couldn't have," said John. "We couldn't possibly all dream the same dream. Anyway—if it's really true we'll find the carpet wet, where the water was spilt from Goldie's bowl last night."

It *was* wet, of course, so they knew it had all really and truly happened. And now they are giving a grand party for the toys!

Real biscuits! Real lemonade poured out of the teapot! Real bits of chocolate! Well—the toys had never enjoyed a party so much before.

Just look at them, having a good time—and even Goldie isn't forgotten. Golly is dropping a bit of biscuit into his bowl!

The Kickaway Shoes

Skip and Jump were very busy brownies. They had been spring-cleaning their cottage from top to bottom—and my, what a lot of rubbish they had turned out!

"Look at that!" said Skip, pointing to an enormous pile of old kettles, old books, and old boots and shoes he had put in their back garden. "Whatever are we going to do with all this rubbish?"

"And look at my pile of rubbish, too!" said Jump. Skip looked. It certainly was an even bigger pile than his. There was a broken-down iron bedstead, two chipped vases, an old enamel candle-stick, four saucepans with holes in—oh, and heaps more things.

"What are we going to do with them?" asked Skip. "We can't burn them; they won't burn."

"And we haven't a dustman in our village," said Jump. "So we can't ask him to collect our rubbish."

"And we are *not* going to throw these old things into the ditches, as lots of untidy people do," said Skip. "That would spoil the countryside. So what *are* we to do?"

"I say—what about borrowing those Kickaway Shoes belonging to old Grumpy Gnome!" cried Jump, all at once. "They would soon take all our rubbish away!"

"Ooh, yes," said Skip. "But I'm afraid of the Grumpy Gnome. He's so bad-tempered, and I don't trust him."

"Well, if we pay him for the loan of his magic shoes, he can't be angry with us," said Jump. "Just think, Skip! Whatever we kick with the Kickaway Shoes immediately disappears! It's wonderful! If I kicked that old saucepan there with a Kickaway Shoe, it would fly away and we'd never see it again! Ooh, it wouldn't take us long to get rid of all our rubbish then, would it?"

"And what fun it would be to do some magic kicking!" cried Skip, jumping about in excitement. "What fun! Let's go and ask Grumpy Gnome now."

"We'll take a piece of gold with us," said Jump, running to his purse, which was on the mantelpiece. "He is sure to charge us a lot. He is a greedy, selfish horrid fellow, and nobody likes him. We won't stay long, in case he puts a nasty spell on us."

Off went the two brownies in great excitement. Jump had the piece of gold safely in his pocket. They soon came to Grumpy's cottage. It was built into the hill-side, and there was a red door with a big black knocker. Jump knocked loudly. Rat-tat-tat!

The Grumpy Gnome opened the door and glared at them. He was a nasty-looking person. He had yellow whiskers and a very long nose. His eyes were small and he wore on his head a round red cap with little silver bells all round the rim. They rang when he walked. It was a magic cap, and he never took it off, not even to brush his hair. So nobody knew whether he had any hair or not.

"What do you want?" he said, in his loud deep voice.

"Please would you lend us your Kickaway Shoes?" asked Jump politely. "We will pay you for the loan of them."

"I shall want a piece of gold," said the Grumpy Gnome, nodding his head till all the silver bells on his cap rang loudly.

"We have brought you a piece," said Jump, and he showed the gold to Grumpy. The gnome's little eyes shone at the sight of the gold, and he suddenly grabbed it and put it into his own pocket.

"Here are the shoes," he said, taking down a curious pair of shoes from a shelf behind the door. They were bright yellow, and had turned-up ends of red-painted iron to kick with. The two brownies took them eagerly. They thanked the gnome and turned to go.

"Bring them back to-night without fail," commanded Grumpy. He shook his head fiercely at them, making all the silver bells tinkle again, and then slammed the door.

"What an unpleasant creature he is, to be sure," said Skip, looking quite pale. "I was really afraid he was going to turn us into black-beetles or something! You know, he is supposed to do that to people he doesn't like. And once he turned a cheeky pixie into a currant bun and ate him! Oooh my, he's a horrid person!"

The brownies hurried home with the magic shoes. When they got there they each put a shoe on their right foot and danced about in glee.

"We've got the Kickaway Shoes, we've got the Kickaway Shoes!" they cried. They made such a noise that Whiskers, their big black cat, came out to see what they were doing.

"Hello, Whiskers, darling!" cried the brownies, who were both very fond of their cat. "Look at our magic shoes."

Whiskers sniffed at them and then hurriedly backed away. She had smelt the magic in them and was afraid. She went off to a corner of the garden.

"Now let's start kicking away all our rubbish!" cried Skip. "Come on! Watch me kick away this old saucepan!"

He stood behind the saucepan, lifted his right foot and gave the saucepan an enormous kick with the iron end of the Kickaway Shoe! Bang!

The saucepan shot into the air and flew away! My, how it flew! The brownies watched it going through the air until it was just a black speck. Then they couldn't see it any longer.

"I wonder where it's gone to," said Jump.

"It's gone to the Land of Rubbish," said Skip. "Now it's your turn, Jump. Kick that vase away!"

Jump kicked with all his might. The vase broke into a hundred pieces, and each piece flew through the air at top speed. They soon disappeared. The brownies giggled. This was great fun!

"We'll both kick away this nasty old bedstead," said Skip. "It's so big it wants two people to kick it, I'm sure!"

They both kicked with all their might. At once the bedstead rose into the air, and to the great delight of the brownies, and to the enormous surprise of the pixies down in the village, the old iron bedstead flew off through the air, looking smaller and smaller the further it flew. It was most exciting.

The brownies laughed till the tears came into their eyes. They were having a glorious time. They kicked away the candle-sticks, the old boots and the tin kettles. They kicked away a pile of books and a broken spade. They kicked dozens of things and shouted in glee when they saw them all flying off in the air, never to come back.

At last there was nothing but an old basket left. Skip gave it a hard kick, and it rose into the air—but oh, goodness, what a dreadful thing! Whiskers, the cat, had curled herself up in that basket and Skip didn't know she was there! When the basket rose up in the air Whiskers shot out and she and the basket flew along together at top speed!

Whiskers mewed loudly, but it was no use. She had to go to the Land of Rubbish, and soon the horrified brownies could see nothing of her but a tiny black speck far away in the sky.

"Oh! Oh!" cried Skip, the tears running down his cheeks in two streams. "I didn't know Whiskers was in the basket! She'll

never come back! Oh, my dear, darling old cat! Oh, Jump, she's gone!"

Jump sobbed, too. Both brownies loved their cat with all their hearts, and it was dreadful to think poor old Whiskers had been kicked off to the Land of Rubbish. How upset she would be! How lonely and frightened!

"Who will g-g-g-give her her m-m-m-m-milk?" wept Skip.

"Who will t-t-t-t-tuck her up in a warm rug at night?" sobbed Jump.

It was dreadful. The brownies couldn't think what to do! They put their arms round one another and cried so much that they made a puddle round their feet.

At last Skip had an idea.

"Let's go to Grumpy Gnome and ask him to tell us how to get Whiskers back!" he said. "There is sure to be a spell to get her back."

"Yes, yes!" cried Jump, wiping his eyes with his big yellow handkerchief. So off they set once more to Grumpy's cottage.

The gnome frowned at them when he opened the door.

"I said bring back the shoes to-night, not this afternoon," he said crossly. "I was just having a nap and you've wakened me."

"Oh, please, Grumpy, we've come about something terribly important," said Skip. "We've kicked Whiskers, our lovely black cat, away by mistake, and we want you to tell us how to get her back!"

Grumpy's little eyes gleamed. "Ha!" he thought. "I can make some money out of this."

"Well," he said, aloud, "That's certainly very serious. You will have to pay me a very large sum of money to get her back. It's very hard to get a black cat back from the Land of Rubbish."

"Oh dear," said Jump and Skip. "How much money do you want?"

"I want fifty pieces of gold!" said Grumpy.

"Ooooooo!" squealed Skip and Jump in horror. "We only have three pieces! Get us our cat back for three pieces, Grumpy."

"Certainly not," said the gnome, pretending that he was shutting the door. "Fifty pieces, or no cat!"

"Wait, wait!" said Jump. "We've only three pieces, I tell you. What else will you take besides our three pieces of gold?"

"Well, I'll take your grandfather clock," said Grumpy.

"Oh!" groaned the brownies sorrowfully. "We do so love our old clock. But you shall have it."

"And your rocking-chair," said Grumpy. "And the pair of lovely brass candle-sticks you have on your mantel-piece."

The brownies groaned again. They were proud of their rocking-chair and candle-sticks. But still, they loved Whiskers more than all these things, so they sadly promised to go back home and fetch the gold, the clock, the chair and the candle-sticks at once.

They ran off, crying. What a dreadful thing to have to give up all their nicest things to the horrid, greedy gnome! If he had been at all kind-hearted he would have been sorry about Whiskers, and would have got her back for nothing. But oh, the Grumpy Gnome had a heart as hard as stone!

Skip and Jump fetched out their big clock, their old rocking-chair, and the two candle-sticks. Skip had the gold in his pocket. He carried the rocking-chair, too. Jump managed to take the grandfather clock and the candle-sticks. They went slowly along, panting and puffing under their heavy loads.

Just as they got near Grumpy's cottage they met Bron, the head brownie of the village. He was most astonished to see Skip and Jump carrying such heavy things.

"Are you moving?" he asked.

"No," said Skip. "We are taking these to Grumpy." Then he told Bron all that had happened, and how Grumpy had made them promise to give him their nicest things in return for getting back Whiskers from the Land of Rubbish.

"So that's why we are taking him our three gold pieces, our beautiful grandfather clock, our rocking-chair and our lovely candle-sticks," said Skip sadly. "But you see, we must get Whiskers back. She'll be so lonely and so frightened."

Bron frowned and looked as black as thunder when he heard about the greed and selfishness of the unkind gnome.

"Where are the Kickaway Shoes?" he asked.

"I've still got one on, and so has Skip,"

said Jump, and he lifted up his right foot to show Bron.

"Give them to me," said Bron.

In great surprise Skip and Jump took off the Kickaway Shoes and watched Bron put them on, one on each foot. Then they looked on in even greater surprise when he marched straight up to Grumpy's front door and banged hard on the knocker.

"RAT-A-TAT-TAT!"

The door flew open and out came Grumpy, looking very angry indeed.

"How dare you knock so loudly!" he began, in a rage—then he stopped when he saw it was Bron knocking and not Skip and Jump.

"I've just come to tell you something, Grumpy Gnome," said Bron, in a very fierce voice. "I've come to tell you that you are the nastiest, greediest, unkindest gnome in the whole of the kingdom, and you don't deserve to live in this nice little village."

"Oh, don't I?" said Grumpy, his little eyes glittering wickedly. "Well, where do I deserve to live then? Tell me that!" And he turned to go indoors again.

"The best place for you is the Land of Rubbish!" shouted Bron, and before Grumpy could get inside his door, he kicked him hard with the iron points of the Kickaway Shoes—first with one shoe and then with the other.

Oh, my goodness me! Grumpy gave a loud yell and rose up into the air, and then, still yelling, he flew on and on to the Land of Rubbish. The brownies watched him—and then suddenly Skip gave a cry.

"Oh, Bron! You've kicked him away before he told us how to get back dear old Whiskers. Oh dear, oh dear!"

"Don't worry!" said Bron cheerfully. "A cat can always find its way home again, no matter where it's taken to. Whiskers will come back all right—and that wicked gnome knew it perfectly well. He was just robbing you of all these things for nothing. Take them back home again, put down a saucer of milk, and wait for Whiskers to come back."

"Oh, thank you, Bron," said the grateful little brownies. "But what are you going to do with the Kickaway Shoes?"

"I shall keep them in my house, and then if anyone wants to borrow them he can do so for nothing," said Bron. He put on his own shoes, and then, taking the Kickaway Shoes under his arm, he went off home, whistling loudly. He stopped every now and then to laugh when he thought of the Grumpy Gnome sailing through the air to the Land of Rubbish!

Skip and Jump staggered home again with all their belongings. They put them back in their places, and then they went to the larder for some milk. They poured out a saucerful, and put it down on the floor, ready for Whiskers when she came back.

Then they put the kettle on for tea, and toasted some muffins, for they really felt very hungry.

And would you believe it, just as they were sitting down to eat their tea, there came a mewing at the door! Skip leapt up and opened it—and there outside was dear old Whiskers, very tired and very hungry, for she had walked a very long way indeed.

"Darling old Whiskers!" cried the brownies in delight, hugging her and stroking her soft fur. "Oh, we are glad to see you! Here's some milk for you! And shall we open a tin of sardines for you, just for a treat?"

They were all so happy that evening. Whiskers sat on Skip's knee first, and then on Jump's, so that they might share her properly between them. She was just as glad to be back again as they were to have her.

As for Grumpy Gnome, he's still in the Land of Rubbish. And a very good place for him, too!

Tit for Tat

Jennifer, the curly-haired doll, had a little hairbrush of her own. She was very proud of it indeed, and the toys liked it too, because it was fun to brush out Jennifer's lovely golden curls at night.

Sometimes she lent it to the toys. Then the teddy-bear brushed his short fur, the golliwog brushed his mop of black hair, the pink cat brushed his coat and the clockwork mouse brushed his whiskers.

The little hairbrush lived in a small box with a little comb. Nobody used the comb because it was very small and it really wasn't any use for combing out Jennifer's thick curls. Sally, the little girl who owned all the toys, never bothered about the hairbrush at all. She hadn't brushed Jennifer's hair once with it, so it was a good thing the toys took turns at brushing it to make it look nice.

Then one day a most annoying thing happened. Sally was turning out her dolls' house and she wanted a brush to sweep the little carpets. She didn't want to borrow Mummy's brush because it was much too big for the tiny carpets.

So you can guess what she did. She borrowed Jennifer's little hairbrush. Just the thing!

"It's fine," said Sally, brushing away at the carpet. "Just right for this job. What a good thing I thought of it."

But the toys didn't think so at all! They looked on in dismay and Jennifer was almost in tears. Her own little hairbrush. How *mean* of Sally!

"Now I shan't be able to brush my hair with it any more," she thought. "It will be dirty and dusty and horrid. Oh, I do think Sally might have used something else. It's too bad of her."

Sally finished brushing the carpets and looked at the little brush. Such hard sweeping had almost worn it out.

"It's no use now," she said. "I'll throw it away." And into the fire it went! Oh, dear! The toys watched it blaze up into flames for a minute or two—and then it was gone!

Jennifer, the curly-haired doll, cried that night. "I did like my little hairbrush," she said. "I've got such a lot of hair that I need a brush for it. Sally never brushes it for me. She doesn't look as if she brushes her own hair, either."

"She's an untidy little girl," said the bear. "She doesn't brush her teeth either. "But she tells her mother that she does. She's a naughty story-teller."

74

"So she is," said the pink cat. "Do you know, her mother gave her a beautiful new green toothbrush last week and Sally hasn't used it yet! She hasn't cleaned her teeth all week."

"Then a toothbrush is just *wasted* on her!" said the clockwork mouse. "It's a pity we can't take it and use it to brush Jennifer's hair each night!"

"Dear me," said the bear, "that's a very fine idea, Mouse! Really very clever indeed. However did you think of it?"

The clockwork mouse would have blushed with delight at this praise if he could. "I don't know how I thought of it," he said. "I must be cleverer than I imagined."

"Shall we get Sally's toothbrush then?" said the pink cat. "I could climb up to the basin in the bathroom and reach up for it, I think. It's in her mug."

"All right. You go then," said the bear, and the pink cat went. He was quite good at jumping. He leapt up to the basin, slithered down into it, climbed up on to the shelf above, took Sally's perfectly new toothbrush in his mouth and jumped down to the floor again.

He padded into the playroom with it. The toys looked at it.

"The handle's too long," said the bear. "Much too long."

"Cut a bit off then," said the pink cat.

"What with?" asked the mouse.

"Sally's got some tools in a box," said Jennifer, the doll. "There's a little saw there. Couldn't we use that?"

Well, they could, of course, and they did! They found the little saw, and the bear sawed away valiantly at the handle of the toothbrush. Everyone watched in excitement.

The end of the handle suddenly fell off. The mouse picked up the little brush in delight. "Its handle is nice and short now," he said. "Just right for a hairbrush. Jennifer, do let me brush your hair for you."

So he was the first to brush the doll's curly hair with the new brush. It brushed beautifully because the bristles were harder than the ones in the hairbrush. Jennifer was delighted.

"Where shall we keep this brush?" asked the bear. "Better not put it into the box because Sally might see it."

"Put it into me," said the little tin teapot, in a spouty voice. "Sally never plays with me now. She'll never look inside me."

So that is where the toys keep the new hairbrush, in case you want to know.

The bear was a little bit worried at first. "Do you think we've done wrong to use Sally's toothbrush?" he said.

"Well, Sally took *my* brush and now we've taken hers, so it's tit for tat," said the curly-haired doll. "Anyway, she never used her toothbrush! We wouldn't have taken it if she did."

I'm just wondering what is going to happen when Sally's mother discovers that Sally's toothbrush is gone. It's going to be *very* difficult for naughty little Sally to make her mother believe that she is cleaning her teeth each night with a toothbrush that isn't there!

The Dumpy Wizard's Party

The Dumpy Wizard was just like his name—fat and round and dumpy. He was a nice old fellow, as merry as a blackbird, and he simply loved giving parties.

People loved going to his parties too! They were so jolly—always lots of nice things to eat and exciting games to play.

But the Dumpy Wizard was very particular about the people he invited to his parties. He wouldn't have anyone with bad manners. He wouldn't have anyone untruthful. He wouldn't have anyone greedy. So, if someone was left out of one of his parties, people always knew that there was something wrong with them just then.

Now one day Tricky the gnome was running down the street, and he turned the corner quickly. Bump! He banged right into Dumpy the Wizard, and they both fell over. Dumpy sat in a puddle. Tricky banged his head against a wall.

"What did you do that for?" roared Dumpy.

"What do you mean?" yelled back Tricky. "You bumped into me as much as I bumped into you!"

"Why don't you look where you are going?" shouted Dumpy.

"I was, but you came where I was just about to go!" cried Tricky.

"Don't be silly," said Dumpy, drying himself with his handkerchief.

"I'm not," said Tricky.

"Oh yes, you are!" said Dumpy.

"Oh no, I'm not!" said Tricky.

"Oh yes, you are!" said Dumpy. "I shan't ask you to my next party."

"I shall come all the same—yes, and eat up your nicest jellies!" said Tricky.

"You won't," said Dumpy.

"Oh yes, I will," said Tricky.

"Oh no, you won't," said Dumpy.

"Now then, move on, you two," said Blueboy, the policeman of the village. "Stop quarrelling!"

So Tricky and Dumpy had to move on. Dumpy was quite sure he *wouldn't* let Tricky come to his party—and Tricky was quite sure he *would* go—and eat up the best jellies too!

Dumpy sent out his invitations—and do you know, *every* one was invited this time—except Tricky, of course! He said *he* didn't care, not he! And in his cunning little head he made a plan.

It was to be a fine party. There was to be a gramophone going, and every one was to sing and dance to it. There were to be four different coloured jellies—green, red, orange and pink—and a fine cake with a rabbit in sugar on the top. Oooh!

The day soon came. Everyone put on his best clothes and looked as excited as could be. Only Tricky kept on his old clothes—but he didn't seem to care a bit—he just ran about as usual, humming and whistling as if *he* didn't care about parties.

Four o'clock came. Gnomes, goblins, brownies, and pixies crowded into Dumpy's little cottage. Only two people were not there—Tricky, of course—and Blueboy the policeman, who had to guard everyone's house because they were all empty.

The gramophone was set going. The dancing began. People sang as they danced. What a noise there was! Everyone was excited and happy, because, set out at the end of the room, was a table full of good things. The four coloured jellies shivered and shook. The sugar rabbit on the iced cake stood up and looked with very sugary eyes at all the dancers. It was a very merry evening.

Just as everyone was feeling hungry, and thinking it was about time the dancing stopped and the eating began, there came a knock at Dumpy's front door.

Blim-blam!

"Who can that be?" said Dumpy, in surprise.

He opened the door. Outside stood someone dressed in a blue uniform, looking very stern.

"Hallo, Blueboy," said Dumpy, in surprise. "What do you want?"

"Have you any idea of the noise you are making?" said Blueboy, in a stern voice.

"Oh, we are only dancing and singing," said Dumpy. "We are not making much noise, Blueboy."

"And I say you *are*!" said Blueboy. "I could hear it very plainly indeed from outside. You may not be able to hear what the noise is like from inside. It sounds really *dreadful* out here! You will wake everyone up!"

"But there is nobody to wake up," said Dumpy. "Everyone is here."

"Don't argue with me, Dumpy," said Blueboy, in such a cross voice that Dumpy was quite surprised. "I tell you that the noise from outside is simply dreadful."

"I'll come out and hear it," said Dumpy. He turned round and called to his guests. "The policeman says that the noise we are making sounds simply dreadful outside. I'm going to hear it."

"You'd better *all* come and hear it!" said the policeman. "Then you will believe what I say. Come along, everyone!"

Blueboy went into the house and pushed everyone out. He shut the door—and once the door was shut, he took off his big helmet—and he wasn't Blueboy at all! He was naughty Tricky, who had dressed up as a policeman to play a joke on Dumpy!

He emptied the four lovely jellies into his helmet, and snatched the sugar rabbit off the cake. Then he slipped quietly out of the kitchen door and ran out of the back garden, home! He had been to the party after all!

The people outside crowded together and listened to hear the dreadful noise that Dumpy's party was supposed to have been making. They listened—and they listened.

"I can't hear a sound!" said Gobbo the pixie.

"Not a word!" said Tippy the gnome.

"The party isn't a bit noisy!" said Dumpy crossly. "I don't know what Blueboy meant. Why, there might be nobody in the house, it's so quiet! There's not a sound to be heard!"

"Well," said Happy the goblin, with a chuckle, "there *is* nobody in the house now—except Blueboy! We've all come out—to listen to ourselves making a noise indoors! Ho, ho, ho!"

"Ho, ho, ho!" roared everyone—and really, it *was* very funny, wasn't it! They had all gone outside to listen to the dreadful noise they were making *in*side! Dear, dear, dear, whatever next!

"Come on in," said Dumpy. "We'll tell that silly old Blueboy we didn't hear a sound!"

So into the house they all went—but where was Blueboy? Nowhere to be found! And where were the four beautiful jellies? Nowhere to be seen! And where, oh, where was that lovely sugar rabbit? He was gone—and the kitchen door was wide open! Oh dear!

"That wasn't Blueboy, it was Tricky!" suddenly cried Dumpy. "Yes, it was. I thought his voice wasn't Blueboy's. Oh, he has been to my party, as he said he would—and taken the best jellies—and my beautiful sugar rabbit too!"

"All because we were foolish enough to do what he told us—and leave the house to hear the noise we were making!" groaned Happy the goblin. "I know, Dumpy—let me run to Tricky's cottage and tell him we've found out his trick—and it was really very funny, you know—and say he can come to the party if he brings back the jellies and the sugar rabbit."

"All right," said Dumpy. "Go and tell him. He is too clever for me—I'd rather he was my friend than my enemy! Goodness knows what he would make us do next!"

So Happy raced off to Tricky's cottage. Tricky had emptied the jellies out of his helmet on to a big dish and was just going to eat them.

"Hi, stop!" said Happy, running in. "We want you to come to the party. That was a clever trick you played, Tricky—but don't make Dumpy unhappy about his jellies and sugar rabbit. He was very proud of them!"

"Very well," said Tricky, getting up. "I'll come—and I'll bring the jellies and the rabbit with me!"

So back he went to the party with Happy—and everyone laughed and said he was a rascal, and Dumpy said he would forgive him if he wouldn't play any more tricks.

So they all settled down again, and the gramophone played, and the jellies were eaten, and the sugar rabbit was put back on the cake, where he looked simply splendid.

"It was a lovely party—even if the jellies *did* taste a bit helmety," said Tricky, when he said good-bye to Dumpy.

"Well—that was *your* fault!" said Dumpy with a grin.

The Sneezing Donkey

Once upon a time there was a small grey donkey who lived in a farm field and ate the grass and the thistles there. As he wandered across the field he felt a tickling in his nose. He lifted up his head and sneezed.

"A-tish-ee-aw!" he sneezed. "A-tish-ee-aw!"

His nose tickled again. He sneezed even more loudly. "A-TISH-ee-aw!"

He blinked and looked round. He could quite well feel another sneeze coming. It came. "A-TISH-EE-TISH-EE-TISH-EE-AW!" he went, so loudly that some geese nearby fled away in alarm.

The donkey looked round, and to his surprise it had begun to pour with rain.

"That was my big sneeze did that," he thought to himself, pleased. "I have made it rain. I am really very clever. I shall tell every one what I have done."

So he cantered over to the sheep and spoke to them. "Sheep, listen to me. Do you see this pouring rain? Well, I made it come when I sneezed so loudly!"

"How clever you are!" said the sheep admiringly. "Nothing happens when *we* sneeze!"

The donkey ran to the old brown horse and spoke to him too. "Horse, listen to me. Do you see this pouring rain? Well, I made it come when I sneezed so loudly."

"How clever you are," said the horse admiringly. "Nothing happens when *I* sneeze!"

The donkey did feel proud. He wondered who else he could tell. He saw the hens and the cock at the end of the field and he trotted over to them. They were sheltering under the big hedge.

"Hens and cock, listen to me. Do you see this pouring rain? Well, I made it come when I sneezed so loudly!"

"How clever you are!" said the hens and the cock admiringly. "Nothing happens when *we* sneeze—but then, we never *do* sneeze!"

The donkey swung his long tail about, and wondered if he could tell any one else. He saw the farm dog lying down in his tub and he cantered over to him.

"Rover, listen to me. Do you see this pouring rain? Well, I made it come by sneezing so loudly."

"How clever of you!" said Rover admiringly. "Nothing happens when *I* sneeze!"

The ducks came waddling by in a row, going to the pond. They were delighted with the rain. The donkey ran over to them.

"Ducks, listen to me," he said. "Do you see this pouring rain? Well, *I* made it come when I sneezed so loudly."

"How clever of you!" said the ducks admiringly. "Nothing happens when *we* sneeze—but how we'd like it to rain whenever we sneeze!"

The donkey was so pleased with himself that he simply didn't know what to do.

The rain went on falling. It rained all day. It rained all night. It went on raining the next day too.

The sheep got tired of the rain. The brown horse got tired of the rain. The hens and the cock got tired of the rain. Rover got tired of the rain. Everywhere was muddy. Everyone was wet and cold. Only the ducks liked the rain.

The sheep, the horse, the hens, cock and dog gathered together by the hedge and grumbled to one another.

"Look what that silly donkey has done with his sneezing! No one would have minded just a shower—but why should he make it rain all day and night like this? Let's go and tell him to stop the rain now."

So they went to the donkey. He was standing under a tree thinking how marvellous it was to have sneezed so much rain down.

"Donkey, we are wet and cold. Stop this rain at once," neighed the horse.

"Donkey, our feathers are dripping. Stop this rain," clucked the hens and cock.

"Donkey, I have a feeling I shall bite your long tail if you don't sneeze again and *stop* the rain!" barked Rover, who could be very fierce.

The donkey stared at every one in alarm. It had been easy enough to begin the rain —but he wasn't at all sure he could stop it. Besides, he couldn't sneeze unless a sneeze came. Whatever was he to do?

"The ducks like the rain," he said at last. "If I stop the rain they will be angry and come and peck me."

"Well, we will be angrier and we will bite you, and nibble you and peck you too!" cried all the animals and birds at once.

"I don't know how to sneeze unless a sneeze happens to come," said the donkey, "and I don't know how to stop the rain."

"Well, why do you start a thing you don't know how to stop?" wuffed Rover crossly. "I shall snap at each of your legs!"

"And I shall butt you with my head," said the sheep.

"And I shall kick you with my heels," said the horse.

"And we will peck you with our beaks," said the birds. So they all began. They were so busy teasing the poor donkey that no one noticed that the clouds were blowing away—and the rain was stopping—and the sun was shining! But that was what was happening. The fields shone and glittered in the sun—it was a really lovely day.

"Stop! Stop!" cried the donkey. "Don't you see the sun? Why are you teasing me like this? The rain has stopped! You ought to be ashamed of yourselves!"

The animals and birds looked round. The donkey was right. It was a beautiful day. The rain had certainly stopped. They all went off joyfully and left the donkey alone in his corner of the field.

"Next time I sneeze I won't say anything about it," said the grey donkey. "Not a single word. There's no pleasing some people! They all said I was so clever, too. Well, maybe I wasn't as clever as I thought I was!"

Next time he sneezed he was *so* surprised to find that no rain came. But *I'm* not surprised—are you?

The Red-Spotted Handkerchief

Raggy the pixie had a red-spotted handkerchief that he was very proud of. It was a big one, with deep red spots all over it. Raggy always wore it in his front coat-pocket, where it stuck out a little so that everyone might see it.

Now one morning as Raggy was going along the road he wanted to sneeze. So he felt for his handkerchief to sneeze into —and it wasn't there!

Raggy was so surprised that he forgot to sneeze, which was a pity, for he really liked a good sneeze. He stood there feeling anxiously in all his pockets, but it wasn't in any of them.

"Somebody must have taken it!" said Raggy. "Yes—somebody at the meeting I've just been to! Oh, how naughty of them! I'll go straight back and see who's got it! They will still be there talking."

So back Raggy went and told everybody at the meeting that he had lost his red-spotted handkerchief.

"You lent it to Gobbo to wipe some spots off his coat," said Tag.

"But I gave it back!" said Gobbo at once.

"And you lent it to Hoppy to wave to his aunt when she passed by the window," said Tag.

"But I gave it back, I know I did!" said Hoppy. He turned out his pockets, and certainly there was no handkerchief there.

"And I lent it to *you*, Tag, to polish your silver watch-chain this morning!" said Raggy. "You must have kept it."

"Indeed I didn't!" said Tag. "I put it back into your pocket myself. Did you lend it to anybody else?"

"Yes, Raggy lent it to me to pop over my head when I went out in the sun to look for Jiggy," said Chuffle. "I tied a knot in each corner—but I untied them when I came back, and gave the hanky back to Raggy. I know I did. It's no use looking at me like that, Raggy. *I* haven't got your hand-kerchief!"

"Well, it's a very funny thing," said Raggy, feeling angry. "I seem to have lent it to all of you this morning, and I haven't got it myself—so *one* of you must have kept it! It's very mean of you!"

"Very well, Raggy, we'll all turn out our

pockets and *show* you that we haven't got it!" said Hoppy. And everyone turned out his pockets for Raggy to see. There were sweets and tops and string and money—but no red-spotted handkerchief.

"Now you turn out *your* pockets, Raggy!" said Hoppy. "We'll make quite sure you're not making all this fuss for nothing!"

So Raggy turned out his pockets, but there was no handkerchief there either.

"It's not a bit of use," said Raggy. "*One* of you has my beautiful handkerchief, and it's very wrong of you!"

"Now, Raggy, when you left the meeting, I *know* I saw your red handkerchief sticking out of your front coat-pocket," said Chuffle. "I just know I did. So if you took it away yourself, *we* couldn't have kept it! Did you meet anyone on your way home?"

"No, nobody!" said Raggy.

"Tell us exactly what you did," said Hoppy.

"Well," said Raggy, "I left the meeting, and I walked up the road. I met a dog with a black head."

"Did you lend *him* your handkerchief?" asked Tag.

"No, of course not," said Raggy. "What would a dog want a handkerchief for? To wave to the engine-driver of the train, or something? Don't be silly."

"Well, go on," said Hoppy.

"And after a bit I saw a cow looking over a hedge," said Raggy.

"Did you lend *her* your handkerchief?" asked Chuffle.

"Really, Chuffle, do you suppose I go about lending cows my handkerchief?" said Raggy. "I suppose you think she wanted to polish her shoes with it? Well, she didn't!"

"Go on. What did you do next?" asked Hoppy.

"Well, let me see," said Raggy. "Oh, I

"It might not be," said Tag. "We'd better look and see if it wants bathing. Turn up your trouser leg, Raggy."

So Raggy had to, and his knee was neatly bound up with—what do you think? Yes—his red-spotted handkerchief!

"I don't wonder you feel ashamed of yourself," said Tag sternly. "Coming back here and making all that fuss, when if only you'd thought for a moment you'd have known quite well where your silly old handkerchief was all the time!"

"I'm sorry," said Raggy, and he went home feeling very much ashamed. He didn't like to wear his handkerchief any more, so now it is neatly folded in his drawer. Silly old Raggy—he did make a mistake, didn't he?

know—a car came suddenly round the corner, and I had to jump quickly into the hedge—and I fell over and hurt my knee very badly."

"Did you really! Poor old Raggy," said Hoppy, for he knew how painful it was to fall down. "Did your knee bleed?"

"Oh, terribly!" said Raggy. "I had to bandage it. I . . ."

He suddenly stopped and went very red indeed. He didn't finish what he was going to say.

"Go on," said Tag.

"Oh, that's all," said Raggy. "Well, I don't think I'll bother any more about my handkerchief. Good-bye, everyone."

"No, no, Raggy, don't go yet!" said Tag, and he held him by the arm. "Let's see your poor hurt knee!"

"Oh, it's quite all right now," said Raggy.

The Toys Go to the Seaside

Once upon a time the goblin Peeko put his head in at the nursery window and cried, "Who wants a day at the seaside?"

The toys sat up with a jerk. They were all alone in the nursery, for Tom and Beryl, whose toys they were, had gone away to stay at their Granny's. The toys were really feeling rather dull. A day at the seaside sounded simply gorgeous!

"How do we go?" asked the pink rabbit.

"By bus," said the goblin grinning. "*My* bus. I bought it yesterday. Penny each all the way there."

"Oooh!" said the sailor doll, longingly. "I *would* like to see the sea. I've never been there—and it's dreadful to be a sailor doll and not to know what the sea is like, really it is!"

"Come on, then," said Peeko. "Climb out of the window, all of you. There's plenty of room in the bus."

So the pink rabbit, the sailor doll, the yellow duck, the walking-doll, the black dog, and the blue teddy bear all climbed out of the window and got into the goblin's bus, which was standing on the path outside. The goblin took the wheel. The bus gave a roar and a jolt that sent the pink rabbit nearly through the roof—and it was off! It was a fine journey to the sea. The goblin knew all the shortest cuts. It wasn't long before the sailor doll gave a yell and cried, "The sea! The sea!"

"Pooh!" said the goblin. "That's just a duck-pond."

"But aren't those gulls sailing on it?" asked the doll.

"No, *ducks*!" said Peeko.

"Quack, quack!" said the yellow toy duck, and laughed loudly at the sailor doll. After that the doll didn't say anything at all, not even when they came to the real sea and saw it glittering and shining in the sun. He was afraid it might be a duck-pond too—or an extra big puddle!

They all tumbled out of the bus and ran on to the beach. "I'm off for a swim!" said the yellow duck.

"I'd like a sail in a boat!" said the sailor doll. "Oh! There's a nice little boat over there, just my size."

It belonged to a little boy. He had gone home to dinner and had forgotten to take his boat with him. The sailor doll ran to it, pushed it out on to the sea, jumped aboard and was soon off for a fine sail. He *was* enjoying himself!

The pink rabbit thought he would like to make himself a burrow in the sand. It was always so difficult to dig a burrow in the nursery. Now he really would be able to make one! So he began to dig, and showered sand all over the blue teddy bear.

"Hi, hi, pink rabbit, what are you doing?" cried the bear. But the pink rabbit was already deep in a sandy tunnel, enjoying himself thoroughly, and didn't hear the bear's shout.

"I shall have a nap," said the blue teddy-bear. "Don't disturb me, anybody."

He lay down on the soft yellow sand and shut his eyes. Soon a deep growly snore was heard. The black dog giggled and looked at the walking-doll. "Shall we bury him in sand?" he wuffed. "He would be so surprised when he woke up and found himself a sandy bear."

"Yes, let's," said the doll. So they began to bury the sleeping teddy in sand. They piled it over his legs, they piled it over his fat little tummy, they piled it over his arms. They didn't put any on his head, so all that could be seen of the bear was just his blunt blue snout sticking up. He did look funny.

"I'm off for a walk," said the walking-doll. "This beach is a good place to stretch my legs. I never can walk very far in the nursery—only round and round and round."

She set off over the beach, her long legs twinkling in and out. The black dog was alone. What should he do?

"The sailor doll is sailing. The yellow duck is swimming. The pink rabbit is burrowing. The teddy-bear is sleeping. The walking-doll is walking. I think I will go and sniff round for a big fat bone," said the black dog. So off he went.

Now when Peeko the goblin came on to the beach two or three hours later, to tell the toys that it was time to go home, do you think he could see a single one? No! There didn't seem to be any one in sight at all! Peeko was annoyed.

"Just like them to disappear when it's time to go home," he said crossly. "Well, I suppose I must just wait for them, that's all. I'll sit down."

Peeko looked for a nice place to sit. He saw a soft-looking humpy bit of sand. It was really the teddy-bear's tummy, buried in the sand, but he didn't know that. He walked over to the humpy bit and sat right down in the middle of it.

The blue bear woke up with a jump.

"Oooourrrrrrr," he growled, and sat up suddenly. The goblin fell over in a fright. The bear snapped at him and growled again. Then he saw it was Peeko.

"What do you mean by sitting down in the middle of me like that?" he said crossly.

"How should I know it was the middle of you when you were all buried in sand?" said Peeko.

"I wasn't," said the bear, in surprise, for he had no idea he had been buried.

"You were," said Peeko.

"I wasn't," said the bear.

"Well, we can go on was-ing and wasn't-ing for ages," said Peeko. "Just tell me this, Teddy—where in the world has every one gone to? It's time to go home."

"Is it really?" said the bear, astonished. "Dear me, it seems as it we've only just come!

"I don't see why you wanted to come at all if all you do is to snore," said Peeko. "Waste of a penny, I call it!"

"Well, if you think that, I won't give you my penny," said the teddy, at once.

"Don't be silly," said the goblin. "Look here, bear, if we don't start soon it will be too late. What am I to do? I'd better go without you."

"Oh no, don't do that," said the bear in alarm. "I'll soon get the others back. We have a special whistle that we use when it's time to go home."

He pursed up his teddy-bear mouth and whistled. It was a shrill, loud whistle, and every one of the toys heard it. You should have seen them rushing back to the beach!

The sailor doll sailed his ship proudly to shore, jumped out, and pulled the ship on to the sand. He really did feel a sailor now!

The yellow duck came quacking and

swimming in, bobbing up and down in delight. She waddled up the beach, and shook her feathers, sending a shower of drops all over Peeko, who was most annoyed.

The walking-doll tore back across the beach. The black dog came running up, carrying an enormous bone in his mouth, very old and smelly. The toys looked at it in disgust.

"Where's the pink rabbit?" asked Peeko. "He *would* be last!"

The toys giggled. Peeko was standing just at the entrance of the pink rabbit's burrow, but he didn't know he was! The toys knew what would happen—and it did!

The pink rabbit had heard the bear's whistling. He was coming back along his burrow. He suddenly shot out, all legs and sand—and Peeko felt his legs bumped hard, and he sat down very suddenly! The pink rabbit had come out in a great hurry, just between the goblin's legs. The toys laughed till they cried. Peeko was quite angry.

"First I sit on a hump that isn't a hump and get a dreadful fright!" he said. "And then I get bowled over by a silly rabbit who comes out of the sand. Get into the bus all of you, before I say I won't take you home."

They all got into the bus. Most of them were tired and sleepy now, all except the teddy-bear, who was very lively indeed— but then, he had been asleep all the time!

They climbed in at the nursery window. They each gave Peeko a penny, and he drove his bus away quietly, and parked it under the lilac bush. The toys crept into the cupboard and sat as still as could be.

And when Tom and Beryl came back the next day from their Granny's they *were* surprised to see how well and brown their toys all looked.

"Just as if they had been to the sea!" said Tom.

"Don't be silly, Tom!" said Beryl.

But he wasn't silly! They *had* been to the sea!

The Little Toy Stove

Angela had a little toy stove. It was a dear little stove, with an oven that had two doors, and three rings at the top to put kettles or saucepans on. At the back was a shelf to warm plates or keep the dinner hot. Angela liked it very much.

But Mother wouldn't let her cook anything on her stove. "No, Angela," she said; "you are not big enough. I am afraid you would burn yourself if you lighted the stove and tried to cook something."

"Oh, but mother, it isn't any fun unless I can cook myself something!" said Angela, nearly crying. But Mother wouldn't let her light the stove, so it was no use saying any more.

Now one day, as Angela was playing with her saucepans and kettles in the garden, filling them with bits of grass for vegetables, and little berries for potatoes and apples, pretending to cook them all for dinner, she heard a tiny voice calling to her.

"Angela! Angela! Do you think you would mind lending me your stove for this evening? My stove has gone wrong, and I have a party. I simply *must* cook for my guests, and so I wondered if you'd lend me *your* stove!"

Angela looked all round to see who was speaking. At last she saw a tiny elf, not more than six inches high, peeping at her from behind a flower.

"Oh!" said Angela in delight. "I've never seen a fairy before. Do come and let me look at you."

The elf ran out from behind the flower. She was dressed in blue and silver, and had long shining wings and a tiny pointed face. Angela thought she was lovely.

"Will you lend me your stove?" asked the elf. "Please say yes."

"Of course!" said Angela. "I'd love to. Will you really cook on it? My Mother won't let me."

"Of course she won't let you," said the elf. "You aren't big enough yet. You might burn yourself."

"Shall I leave my stove here for you?" asked Angela.

"Yes, please," said the elf. "I can easily cook out here. It is to be an open-air party. I live behind those big hollyhocks, so I shan't have far to bring my things."

"I suppose I couldn't come and watch you?" said Angela longingly. "I've never seen my toy stove really doing cooking, you know!"

"Well, you come and watch to-night," said the elf. "I shall begin my cooking at nine o'clock. The party begins at eleven."

Angela was so excited when she went in to bed. She meant to put on her dressing-gown and get up at nine o'clock, and creep down the garden. So she lay awake until she heard the hall clock chime nine. Then up she got and slipped down the stairs and out of the garden door.

She could quite well see where her toy stove was, because smoke was rising from it. The elf had got it going well. A lovely smell of baking and roasting came on the air. Oooh!

You should have seen the elf cooking on that stove. The oven was full of things roasting away well. The plates were getting nice and hot in the plate-rack!

"Just listen to my pudding boiling away in that saucepan," said the elf, pleased. "This stove cooks very well indeed, it's a fine stove."

"What sort of pudding is it?" asked Angela.

"It's a tippy-top pudding," said the elf. "And I'm cooking a poppity cake too and some google buns."

"Oh my, they do sound delicious," said Angela; "and so exciting! I've never heard of them before. I suppose I couldn't come to the party?"

"No," said the elf. "It is too late a party for little girls like you. But, Angela, as I think it is really very kind of you to let me use your lovely stove for my cooking, I'd like you to taste some of my dishes. Listen! There is sure to be some tippy-top pudding, some poppity cake, and a few google buns over after the party. If there are I will put them on a plate and leave them inside the oven. See? I will clean the stove nicely, too, and leave it all shiny and bright. Now, good night, dear. You must go to bed. You are yawning."

"Good night!" said Angela, and she ran off. In the morning she went to see if there *was* anything inside her oven. And what do you think? There was a neat little blue dish, and on one side of it was a slice of yellow tippy-top pudding, and on the other side were three google buns, red and blue, and a large slice of green poppity cake! Ooooh!

Angela ate them all—and they were simply delicious. She *does* so hope the elf will want to borrow her stove again. Wouldn't it be lovely if she did?

Sally Simple's Spectacles

Sally Simple had a fine pair of spectacles. They sat on her round nose beautifully, and looked very grand, for the glass was square, not round, and the frame was bright green. Sally Simple felt very fine indeed when she wore her spectacles. She didn't really need to wear any, for her eyes were perfectly good—but when she had seen those grand green spectacles in a shop, with their square glass, she had fallen in love with them and had bought them!

One day Sally went to a sewing-meeting. She set off, in her best green blouse with the yellow buttons, and her spectacles in a case. It was raining hard, so Sally put up her umbrella and went squelching through the mud.

There were a lot of people at the sewing-meeting. Old Dame Twinkle was there, and Mother Hubbard. Mrs. Pippitty was there and Mrs. Popoff. The meeting was quite crowded. Sally Simple was pleased.

"There will be all the more people to see my beautiful glasses," she thought to herself. She sat down at a table, and put her umbrella beside her, for she was always afraid that some one else might take it if she put it into the umbrella stand.

Sally took out her spectacle case and opened it. She put her marvellous green spectacles on her round nose and looked to see if any one was admiring them.

"Goodness, Sally!" said Dame Twinkle, her shining face all over smiles, "what do you want spectacles for? Your eyes are as good as mine any day!"

"And what queer ones they are!" said Mother Hubbard.

"They cost a lot of money," said Sally Simple, offended. "They are the very latest fashion. Your bonnet, Mother Hubbard, is much queerer than my spectacles. It must be more than fifty years old."

"Now, now!" said Mrs. Popoff. "No quarrelling, please. I am sure, Sally, that your spectacles will help you to sew beautifully!"

Sally put her glasses firmly on her nose and bent over her work. "Everyone is jealous of me because I have such fine spectacles," she thought. "Well, let them be!"

Now Sally soon found that she could see better without the new spectacles than with. They were not made for *her* eyes, and they hurt them. What a nuisance! Sally began to blink and wink—but she did not want to take them off—no! What would be the good of buying them if she didn't wear them?

But when tea-time came Sally Simple took them off and put them on the table. She did like to see properly all that she was eating. She ate tomato sandwiches and cucumber sandwiches. She ate brown bread and butter and strawberry jam. She ate a ginger bun, a chocolate cake, and two slices of cherry cake—and she drank four cups of tea. So she enjoyed herself very much, and laughed and joked with the rest.

But when tea was over, Sally thought she would put her beautiful glasses on again, and she looked for them—but, dear me, they were gone!

"I put them on the table, just here!" said Sally Simple, and she looked everywhere on the table for her lovely glasses. But they weren't there! She looked in the cotton box. She looked among the scissors. She unrolled the roll of cloth nearby. But nowhere could she see her precious glasses!

"Has somebody taken my glasses?" asked Sally in a loud voice. "They are gone! I simply must have them to wear whilst I am sewing."

"*I* haven't seen them," said Mother Hubbard.

"Nor have I," said Dame Twinkle.

"I expect Sally's got them herself," said Mrs. Pippitty. "Have you looked in your pocket, Sally?"

"Of course, I have," said Sally. "I've looked everywhere!"

"They may be on the floor," said Mrs. Popoff. So everyone put down scissors, sewing, and needles, and hunted on the floor for Sally's spectacles. But they were nowhere to be seen. It was really most mysterious. The empty case was in Sally's pocket—but the glasses seemed to have disappeared completely.

"There is only one thing I can think," said Sally, pursing her lips.

"And what is that?" asked Dame Twinkle.

"Well—I think *one* of you has taken my new spectacles," said Sally. "I know *some* people felt jealous of them! Now, who is it? I tell you, I must really have them back, because they cost a lot of money."

"Sally! You should not say that one of us has taken your silly glasses," said Mother Hubbard crossly.

"They are *not* silly," said Sally.

"They are—*very*!" said Mother Hubbard.

"They are *not*!" said Sally, going red.

"Now, now!" said Mrs. Popoff. "I expect they will turn up soon. Shall we all open our work-bags and see if the glasses have got in there by mistake?"

So everyone opened her basket and tipped out cottons and silks and needles —but nobody had those glasses, it seemed. It was most peculiar.

"Well, I simply don't know where they can have gone to, Sally," said Mrs. Pippitty. "Let us get on with our work again now. We have wasted quite enough time."

"Well, I shall not stay here a minute more," said Sally Simple in a rage. "*Some one* has my glasses—my beautiful green glasses—and I shall go home and not come to this horrid, nasty sewing-meeting any more!"

"Don't be silly, Sally," said Mother Hubbard.

But Sally's mind was made up. She was not going to stay and sew without her glasses! She got up from her seat and took down her mackintosh from its peg. She put it on, and buttoned it right up to her neck. She set her hat straight. She put on her gloves and buttoned them. Then she took up her umbrella and walked to the door.

"Sally, don't go in a temper like this," said Mrs. Popoff kindly. "It is foolish of you. Your glasses will turn up somewhere, and then you will be sorry."

"I shall *not* be sorry!" said Sally, who was most upset. She opened the door. It was pouring with rain. Dear, dear, what wet weather!

"And I hope that whoever has my glasses will be WELL PUNISHED!" said Sally. She opened her umbrella—and oh, my goodness me, out of it fell something that shone and glittered—something that fell to the ground—and smashed into a hundred shining little pieces—Sally's beautiful green glasses!

They had slipped off the table into her umbrella, as it stood by her knee at tea-time. No one had seen them slip off—and no one had thought of looking in Sally's own umbrella! Every one stared—and stared.

"Well, Sally," said Mother Hubbard, at last, "your wish has come true. You said that you hoped that whoever had your glasses would be well punished—and you were the one that had them—and you have been punished because they have broken."

Poor Sally Simple! She did feel so ashamed of herself—and there were her lovely glasses, smashed to bits—all because she had walked out in a temper! Tears poured down Sally's cheeks. Kind Mrs. Popoff saw them and came running to Sally. She put her arms round her.

"Never mind," she said. "You look *so* much nicer without spectacles, Sally, dear. And besides, I am sure they were bad for your eyes, because they made you wink and blink. So don't worry any more. Come and take your things off again, and do a bit more sewing."

Sally was so ashamed of herself that all she wanted to do was to go home—but Mrs. Popoff was so kind that she went back again into the room and took off her things.

"I beg everybody's pardon," she said in a little voice. "It was very foolish and wrong of me."

And after that Sally Simple didn't buy any more spectacles—because her eyes really were very good indeed. She is much nicer now, so perhaps it was a good thing those green glasses were smashed to bits. What do *you* think?

The Ho-Ho Goblins

Once upon a time the Ho-Ho goblins laid a plan. They wanted to catch the Skippetty pixies, but for a long time they hadn't been able even to get near them. Now they had thought of a marvellous idea!

"Listen!" said Snicky, the head goblin. "You know when the pixies sit down to feast, in the middle of their dancing, don't you? Well, they sit on toadstools! And if *we* grow those toadstools we can put a spell in them so that as soon as the pixies sit down on them, they shoot through the earth into our caves below—and we shall have captured them very nicely indeed!"

"A splendid idea!" said the other goblins in delight. "We'll do it!"

"Leave it all to me," said Snicky. "I will go to them and offer to grow them toadstools for their dance much more cheaply than any one else—and I will grow them just over our caves, as I have said—then the rest is easy."

So the goblins left it to Snicky. As soon as he heard that the invitations to the party had been sent out, he went knocking at the the door of Pinky, one of the chief pixies.

"What do you want?" asked Pinky, opening the door. She did not like the Ho-Ho goblins.

"Dear Madam Pinky," said Snicky, bowing low, "I come to ask you if you will kindly allow me to grow the toadstools for you for your dance."

"How much do you charge?" asked Pinky.

"One gold piece for one hundred toadstools," said Snicky.

"That is very cheap," said Pinky. "We had to pay three gold pieces last time."

"Madam, they will be excellent toadstools, strong and beautiful," said Snicky. "Please let the Ho-Ho goblins do them for you."

"Well, I don't like the goblins, but that's no reason why I shouldn't have their toadstools," said Pinky. "Very well. You shall make them for our dance. We want them in the wood under the oak tree."

"Madam, it is very damp there," said Snicky. "It would be better to grow them under the birch tree."

Snicky knew quite well that under the birch tree lay the caves of the Ho-Ho goblins. He must grow the toadstools there, or the goblins would not be able to capture the pixies as they had planned.

"Oh, very well," said Pinky. "It can't make much difference whether the dance is held under the oak or the birch. We want the toadstools on the next full-moon night, Snicky."

Snicky ran off full of glee. He had got what he wanted! He called a meeting of the others, and told them.

"Now," he said, "not one of you must tell a word of this to anyone, for we must keep it a secret. We must get a runaway spell from Witch Grumple, and each toadstool must be rubbed with the spell. Then, at a magic word, all the toadstools, with the pixies on them, will rush away through the ground straight to our caves below."

"Hurrah!" cried the Ho-Ho goblins. "They will be our servants at last."

Snicky went to ask Witch Grumple for the spell. She was not at home. Her servant, a big black cat with green eyes, said that his mistress had gone walking through the fields to collect some dew shining in the new moon.

"I'll go and meet her," said Snicky. So off he went. He found the witch walking by the hedges that ran round the ripening cornfield. She had a dish in which she was collecting the silvery dewdrops.

"Good evening, Witch Grumple," said Snicky. "May I speak secretly with you for a moment?"

"Certainly," said the witch. She looked all around to see that no one was about. "Come into the corn," she said. "No one will hear us then. What is it you want?"

"I want a runaway spell," said Snicky.

"What will you give me for it?" asked the witch.

"I'll give you two Skippetty pixies for servants," said Snicky.

"Don't be silly," said Grumple. "You haven't any pixies to give away!"

The corn heard it with its many, many ears! Grumple had quite forgotten that corn has ears. They were ripe ears too, ready to catch the slightest whisper. They listened to all that Snicky said, and, because they liked the Skippetty pixies, they wanted to warn them. So the next time the wind blew the corn, it whispered its secret to the breeze.

"Shish-a-shish-a-shish-a-shish!" went the corn as the wind blew over it. The wind understood its language and listened in astonishment to the tale the corn told of Snicky's plan. Off it went to the pixies at once.

When Pinky heard of Snicky's plan, she went pale with rage and fear. To think how that horrid, horrid goblin had nearly tricked her! Off she sped to the Fairy King and told him everything. He laughed and said, "Aha! Now we shall be able to play a nice little trick on Snicky himself!"

So, on the night of the dance, all the pixies laughed and talked as if they had no idea of the toadstool trick. The goblins crept around, watching and waiting for the moment when they could send the toadstools rushing down below to their caves.

Suddenly Pinky stopped the dance and said, "Let's play musical chairs for a change! Goblins, come and play with us!"

The Ho-Ho goblins felt flattered that they should be asked to play with the pixies. So they all came running up. Pinky pointed to the toadstools that Snicky had grown for them.

"Those shall be the chairs," she said. "When the music stops, every one must sit down if he can!"

"I soon shall have, if you let me have the runaway spell," said Snicky.

"Tell me what you are going to do with it," said Grumple.

"No," said Snicky; "someone might hear me."

"There is no one to hear you," said Grumple. "Tell me, or I will not let you have the spell."

So Snicky told Grumple exactly what he was going to do to capture the pixies, and she shook with laughter.

"Splendid!" she said. "I shall be glad to see those stuck-up little pixies punished. Come back with me and I'll give you the spell."

Now all would have gone well with the

Ho-Ho goblin's plan—if someone hadn't overheard the secret that Snicky told Grumple. Who heard it? You will never guess.

The band began again. Pixies and goblins ran merrily round the toadstools—but every pixie had been warned not to sit down, but to let the goblins take the toadstools. So, when the music stopped, the goblins made a rush for the toadstools and sat heavily down on them meaning to win the game of musical chairs.

As soon as Pinky saw the goblins sitting on the toadstools, she called out a magic word at the top of her voice. Those toadstools sank down through the ground at top speed! You see, Snicky had rubbed them hard with a runaway spell the night before—and Pinky knew the word to set them off!

To the goblin's great fright, the toadstools rushed down to their cave—and there, calmly waiting for them, were the soldiers of the Fairy King. As the toadstools came to rest in the caves, each goblin was surrounded by three soldiers. They were prisoners!

"That was a fine trick you planned, wasn't it?" grinned a soldier. "But not so fine when it's played on yourselves! Come along now, quick march!"

Off the goblins went—and for a whole year they had to work hard for the pixies, to punish them for trying to play such a horrid trick.

And to this day they don't know who gave their secret away—although people say that if you listen to the corn as it whispers in the wind, you can, if you have sharp ears, hear it telling the wind all about Witch Grumple and Snicky the goblin. I'd love to hear it, wouldn't you?

Poor Captain Puss!

Ronald and Jill were very lucky. In the summer they always went to Cliffsea, where their father had a house almost on the beach. It was such fun to wake up in the morning and hear the waves splashing on the sands not far off.

All the household went to Cliffsea in the summer, even Toby the dog and Patter the kitten! No one was left behind. Toby liked the sea very much, and Patter loved playing about in the sand.

Next door to the children's house was a smaller one, and two cats and a dog lived there with their mistress. The dog was called Spot, and the cats were called Sooty and Snowball, so you can guess what they were like to look at.

Toby, Patter, Sooty, Snowball, and Spot were soon good friends. Patter the kitten had a fine time with them. They made quite a fuss of her because she was the smallest and youngest.

So she was rather spoilt, and she became vain and boastful. Ronald and Jill spoilt her too, and said she was just the cleverest kitten they had ever seen.

"See how she runs after my ball!" said Ronald, as Patter raced over the sand to get his ball.

"See how Patter plays with this bit of seaweed!" said Jill. "She fetched it off the rocks for me, Ronald. She *is* a clever kitten! She can do simply anything."

Patter felt very clever indeed. She went about with her head in the air and began to think that the other animals were rather stupid.

But there was one thing she would *not* do! She wouldn't go paddling and bathing with the children as Toby and Spot did. No—she hated the water. She thought it was simply horrid to get her dainty little feet wet.

Then one day Ronald and Jill brought down a beautiful big ship to the beach. It was a toy one, but was so big that Toby and Spot could almost get into it. Ronald and Jill played happily with it all the morning, and sailed it on the rock-pools that were spread all over the beach.

When they went indoors to dinner the five animals crowded round the pretty boat.

"I wish I could sail in it!" said Toby. "I'd love to sail over that pool. I would make a good captain!"

"So would I," said Spot, wagging his tail and sniffing at the boat as it stood half-upright in the sand.

"I would make the *best* captain!" said Patter the kitten boastfully. "Ronald and Jill are always saying what a clever kitten I am. I am sure I could sail this ship much better than any of you!"

"Why, Patter, you little story-teller!" cried Snowball, "you know how you hate to get your feet wet! You wouldn't be any good at all at sailing a boat."

"Yes, I should," said Patter crossly. "I know just what to do. You pull that thing there—the tiller, it's called—and the boat goes this way and that. I heard Ronald say so!"

"You don't know anything about it at all," said Sooty scornfully. "You are just showing off as usual!"

"I'm not!" mewed Patter angrily. She jumped into the boat and put her paw on the tiller. "There you are," she said. "This is what makes the boat go!"

The others laughed at her. They were sure that Patter would hate to go sailing really. They ran off and left her. She stared after them crossly, and then she lay down in the boat in the warm sunshine. She wouldn't go and play with the others if they were going to be so horrid to her. No, they could just play by themselves!

Patter shut her eyes, for the sun was very bright. She put her nose on her paws and slept. She didn't hear the sea coming closer and closer. She didn't know the tide was coming in! It crept up to the boat. It shook it a little. But Patter slept on, dreaming of sardines and cream.

Toby, Spot, Sooty and Snowball wondered where Patter was. They couldn't see her curled up in the ship. They thought she had gone indoors in a huff.

"She is getting to be a very foolish little kitten," said Toby. "We must not take so much notice of her."

"It is silly of her to pretend that she would make such a good sailor," said Sooty. "Every one knows that cats hate the water."

"Well, we won't bother about her any more," said Snowball. "She's just a little silly. Let's lie down behind this shady rock and have a snooze. I'm sleepy."

So they all lay down and slept. They were far away from the tide and were quite safe.

But Patter was anything but safe! The sea was all round the ship now! In another minute it would be floating! A great big wave came splashing up the beach—and the ship floated! There it was, quite upright, floating beautifully!

The rock-pool disappeared. It was now part of the big sea. The ship sailed merrily on it. It bobbed up and down on the waves.

Patter suddenly woke up, and wondered why things bobbed about so. She sat up and saw that she had fallen asleep in the boat—and when she looked over the side, what a shock for her! She was sailing on the sea! Big waves came and went under the boat. The beach was far away!

"Miaow!" wailed Patter. "Miaow! I'm out at sea! I'm afraid! I shall drown!"

But no one heard her. The sea was making such a noise as the tide came in. Patter forgot how she had boasted about being a good sailor. She forgot that she had boasted she could sail the boat quite well. She just clung on to the side and watched with frightened eyes as the green waves came and went.

Ronald and Jill suddenly remembered that they had left their sailing ship on the beach.

"My goodness! And the tide's coming in!" said Ronald in dismay. "Quick, Jill, we must go and see if our boat is safe!"

They ran from the house to the beach—and then saw the tide was right in. And, far away, on the big waves, floated their beautiful ship, all by itself!

"Look!" cried Jill. "There it is! But there is someone in it. Who is it, Ronald?"

Ronald stared hard. Then he shouted out in surprise: "Why, it's Patter the kitten! Yes, it really is! Look at her in the boat, Jill!"

"Oh, the clever thing!" cried Jill, who really thought that the kitten was sailing the ship. "Oh, whoever heard of a kitten sailing a boat before! Spot, Toby, come and look at Patter sailing our ship!"

Spot, Toby, Sooty and Snowball awoke

just when the tide was coming in," said Sooty.

"All the same, she's very frightened," said Snowball, who had heard two or three frightened mews.

"Sail the boat to shore, Patter!" shouted Ronald. "Sail her in! We don't want to lose her!"

But Patter was much too frightened to pay any attention to what was said. She just went on clinging to the side of the boat. She felt very ill, and wished that she was on dry land.

Spot was quite worried. He knew what a little silly Patter really was—but all the same he thought she had been frightened

in a hurry and ran to see what all the excitement was about. When they saw Patter the kitten out in the boat, rocking up and down on the sea, they could hardly believe their eyes.

"Captain Puss is sailing the boat," said Jill. "Captain Patter Puss! Isn't she clever!"

But Spot didn't think that Patter was as clever as all that. His sharp ears had caught a tiny mew—and that mew was very, very frightened. It wasn't the voice of a bold captain—it was the mew of a terrified kitten!

"I believe she went to sleep in the boat and the tide came and took it away," wuffed Spot to Toby.

"Well, it will do her good to see that she isn't such a marvellous captain after all!" Toby barked back.

"She *would* be silly enough to fall asleep

quite enough. What could be done?

"I'll go and fetch her," wuffed Spot, and he plunged into the sea. He swam strongly through the waves, which were now getting quite big, for the wind had blown up in the afternoon. Up and down went Spot, swimming as fast as he could, for he was really rather afraid that the ship might be blown over in the wind—and then what would happen to Patter!

The boat was a good way out. The wind blew the white sails strongly. The waves bobbed it up and down like a cork. Patter was terribly frightened, for once or twice she thought the boat was going over.

And just as Spot got there, the wind gave the sails such a blow that the boat *did* go over! Smack! The sails hit the sea, and the boat lay on its side. Splash! Poor Patter was thrown into the water. She couldn't swim—but Spot was there just in time! He caught hold of her by the skin of her neck, and holding her head above the water, he swam back to shore. The ship lay far out to sea on its side.

Spot put poor, wet, cold Patter on the sand, and shook himself. Patter mewed weakly.

The others came running up to her.

"Well, you didn't make such a good sailor after all," said Sooty.

"Don't say unkind things now," said Snowball. "Patter has been punished enough. Come into the house, Patter, and sit by the kitchen fire and dry yourself."

Ronald and Jill watched the five animals running into the house. Then Ronald turned up his shorts and went wading into the water to see if he could get back his boat.

"That kitten was silly!" he said. "She took my boat out to sea, couldn't sail it back again, made it flop on to its side, and fell out herself! She isn't so clever as she thinks."

He got back his boat and went to dry the sails in the kitchen. Patter was there, sitting as close to the fire as she could, getting dry.

"Hullo, Captain Puss!" said Ronald. "I don't think you are much of a sailor!"

"No, she is just a dear, silly little kitten," said Jill.

Patter felt ashamed. How she wished she hadn't boasted about being a good sailor! She wondered if others would ever speak to her again.

They did, of course, and as soon as they found that she wasn't boastful any more they were as good friends as ever.

But if Patter forgets, they laugh and say, "Now, Captain Patter! Would you like to go sailing again?"

The House in the Tree

Eileen and Marigold lived next door to one another, and they played together every day. But they were quite different!

Eileen was lazy and wouldn't bother about anything. Marigold liked to work hard, and would help anyone if she could. Eileen was eight and Marigold was seven. Eileen couldn't read and Marigold could. Eileen didn't know even her twice times table, but Marigold had already got as far as four times.

Eileen laughed at Marigold because she liked doing things. "You are silly to learn to read," she said. "Your mother won't read to you any more now."

"Oh yes, she will," said Marigold; "and I'll be able to read to myself, too, so I'll get twice as many stories!"

"Well, I can always get my mother to read to me whenever I want a story," said Eileen. "So what's the use of bothering to learn?"

"You are lazy," said Marigold. "You can't even knit, as I can—you can't even tie a bow!"

"Well, you couldn't last week!" said Eileen.

"But I can now," said Marigold. "Look—I tied my own shoe-laces this morning—one on each foot. It took me a long time, but I did it. Now I can tie them every morning."

"Pooh!" said Eileen, scornfully. "I can get my mother to tie mine in half the time. What's the use of learning that if you've got someone to do it for you?"

Now one day, when Eileen and Marigold were playing in the wood, they heard the sound of someone squealing.

"Ooooh! Ooooh! Now look what I've done!"

Eileen and Marigold peeped round a tree to see who was squealing—and they saw a plump little woman sitting on a tree-trunk sucking her hand.

"What have you done?" asked Marigold.

"I was chopping wood for my fire when the chopper cut my thumb," said the little woman, her bright eyes twinkling at Marigold. "I shall have to bandage it."

"I'll do it for you," said Marigold. She took her clean hanky from her pocket and tore it into neat strips for a bandage. Then she quickly bound up the little woman's thumb, and tied a neat little bow.

"What beautiful bows you tie," said the little woman, looking at her bandage. "Thank you very much. My goodness, my thumb does hurt. I don't believe I'll be able to dress my children for their party this afternoon!"

"Shall we help you?" asked Marigold.

"*I* don't want to," said Eileen, who was feeling lazy. "I want to play."

"Can you tie bows?" the little lady asked her, and Eileen shook her head. "Well, it's no use coming to help dress my children if you can't tie bows, because their party dresses have sashes—and they have to be tied in beautiful bows and each child has two plaits with bows at the end. So *you* wouldn't be any help. But this little girl would be a great help. Come along in, my dear!"

"Where's your house?" asked Marigold, looking round.

"In here!" said the little woman, and she pressed a bit of bark on a great oak-tree. A round door swung open! Marigold stared in surprise. So did Eileen. The little woman went in at the door and pulled Marigold in too. The door shut with a bang.

There was such a dear little room inside the tree. It was quite round. There was a table in the middle and a wooden seat ran all round. Seven small pixie children were sitting on the seat, as quiet as mice.

"Oh!" said Marigold, "your children are fairies!"

"Yes," said the little woman, and she shook out a pair of wings from under her shawl. "I'm a pixie too, but I usually cover up my wings in the wood in case anyone sees me. Now, children—get your dresses!"

Each child opened a tiny cupboard beneath the seat where she sat and pulled out gossamer dresses. They were in two colours—blue—and yellow. The blue dresses had yellow sashes and the yellow dresses had blue sashes. Each child had two pieces of hair ribbon to match her sash. They all wore plaits and looked perfectly sweet.

What a busy time Marigold had! She tied seven sashes into beautiful bows! She tied fourteen hair-ribbons into fourteen bows on the ends of fourteen little plaits! The children were as good as gold. Their mother was so grateful to Marigold.

"I suppose you wouldn't take the children to their party for me, would you?" she asked. "My hurt thumb really makes me feel rather ill."

"Oh, I'd *love* to!" said Marigold at once. "Where is the party?"

"It is at the Princess Silvertoes' palace in the heart of the wood," said the little woman. "The children know the way. Tell the Princess about my thumb, won't you, and say I'm sorry I cannot come. Good-bye, dears!"

They all went out of the tree. Eileen was still outside, wondering what had happened to Marigold. When she saw her coming out with seven beautifully dressed pixies she was most surprised.

"I'm taking these pixies to a party at Princess Silvertoes', in the heart of the wood," said Marigold to Eileen. "Go home and tell Mother I will be a bit late."

"I want to come too," said Eileen in excitement.

"Well, you can't," said the pixies' mother, standing in the doorway. "You didn't want to help me at all. You can't even tie a bow! You are a lazy, good-for-nothing little girl, and I don't want you to go with my children. Go home!"

So whilst Marigold went to the party and had a wonderful time, poor Eileen had to go home in tears. And I shouldn't be surprised if she learnt to tie a bow the very next day! I hope *you* can tie a bow—you never know when it will come in useful, do you?

Jinky the Jumping Frog

Jinky was a little green jumping frog who lived in the toy cupboard with all the other toys. He had a spring inside him that made him able to jump high up in the air, and he often frightened the toys by his enormous jumps. He didn't *mean* to frighten them, but, you see, he couldn't walk or run, so his only way of getting about was to jump.

"I'm sorry if I startle you," he said to the angry toys. "Please try and get used to my big hops. I can't do anything else, you see."

The toys thought he was silly. He was a shy little frog, and he didn't say much, so the toys thought he was stupid. They left him out of all their games at night, and he was often very lonely when he sat in a corner of the toy cupboard and watched the toys playing with one of the nursery balls.

Now the prettiest and daintiest of all the toys was Silvertoes, the fairy doll. She was perfectly lovely, and she had a silver crown on her head, a frock of finest gauze that stood out all round her, a pair of shining silver wings, and a little silver wand which she always carried in her right hand. Everyone loved her, and the green frog loved her most of all.

But she wouldn't even look at him! He had once made her jump by hopping suddenly down by her, and she had never forgiven him. So Jinky watched her from a distance and wished and wished she would smile at him just once. But she never did.

One night there was a bright moon outside, and the brownie who lived inside the apple tree just by the nursery window came and called on the toys.

"Let's all go out into the garden and dance in the moonlight," he said. "It's lovely and warm, and we could have a fine time together."

Out went all the toys through the window! They climbed down the apple-tree, and slid to the grass below. Then they began to dance in the moonlight. They all took partners except the green frog, who was left out. He sat patiently on the grass, watching the other toys, and wishing that he could dance too.

There was such a noise of talking and laughing that no one noticed a strange throbbing sound up in the sky. No one, that is, except the green frog. He heard it and he looked up. He saw a bright silver aeroplane, about as big as a rook, circling round and round above the lawn.

Then someone looked down from the aeroplane and Jinky shivered with fright— for who should it be but Sly-One, the gnome who lived in Bracken Country, far away. He was a sly and unpleasant person, and nobody, fairy or toy, liked to have anything to do with him.

"I wonder what he wants to come here for to-night!" said Jinky to himself. "He's up to some mischief, I'm sure!"

He was! He suddenly swooped down in his aeroplane, landed near the toys, ran up to the fairy doll, snatched her away from the teddy bear who was dancing with her, and ran off with her to his aeroplane!

How she screamed! "Help! Help! Oh, please save me, toys!"

The toys were so astonished that they stood and gaped at the bold gnome. He threw the fairy doll into his aeroplane, jumped in himself, and away he went into the air! Then the toys suddenly saw what was happening, and began to shout.

"You wicked gnome! Bring her back at once! We'll put you in prison if you don't!"

The gnome felt quite safe in the air. He circled round and round the toys and bent over the side of his aeroplane to laugh at them.

"Ha, ha!" he said. "Put me in prison, did you say? Well, come and catch me!"

To the great anger of the toys he flew very low indeed, just above their heads. The teddy bear, who was tall, tried to jump up and hang on to the aeroplane, but he couldn't quite reach it. He was in despair.

"Whatever shall we do?" he cried to the toys. "We can't possibly rescue the fairy doll in that horrid aeroplane."

"Ha, ha!" laughed the gnome again, swooping down to the toys—and just at that moment the green frog saw his chance! He would do a most ENORMOUS jump and see if he could leap right on to the aeroplane.

He jumped. My goodness me, what a leap that was! You should have seen him! He jumped right up into the air, and reached out his front feet for the aeroplane. And he just managed it! He hung on to the tail of the 'plane, and then managed to scramble up. The gnome had not seen him.

The toys were too astonished to say a word. They stood with open mouths looking up at the brave green frog, and he signed to them to say nothing about him. He thought that if the gnome did not know he was there he might be able to rescue the fairy doll without much difficulty.

The gnome flew off in his aeroplane. He wanted to reach Bracken Cottage that night, and he meant to marry the fairy doll in the morning. He thought it would be lovely to have such a pretty creature cooking his dinner and mending his clothes.

The frog crouched down on the tail of the aeroplane. It was very cold there, but he didn't mind. He was simply delighted to think that he would have a chance to do something for the pretty fairy doll.

At last Sly-One arrived at Bracken Cottage. He glided down and landed in the big field at the back of his house. Out he jumped, and turned to the fairy doll, who was cold, frightened and miserable.

"Wait here a minute and I'll just go and unlock the door," he said. "Then I'll come back and fetch you." He ran off—and as soon as he had gone the green frog hopped down into the seat beside the fairy doll.

She nearly screamed with fright, but he stopped her.

"Sh!" he said. "It's only me, Jinky the jumping frog. I've come to save you. Do you think we can fly back in this aeroplane?"

"Oh, Jinky, I'm so glad to see you," sobbed the poor doll. "Look, you jerk that handle up, and the aeroplane should fly up into the air."

Jinky jerked the handle in front of him, but nothing happened. The gnome had stopped the engine, and of course, it wouldn't move. Jinky was in despair. He didn't in the least know how to fly the 'plane, and he was terribly afraid that if it did begin to fly there would be an accident.

"It's no good," he said, hopping out of the seat. "I can't make it go. Come on, fairy doll, get out, and jump on my back. I'll leap off with you, and perhaps we can escape that way."

"Take the handle out of the aeroplane," said the doll. "Then that nasty gnome can't fly after us in it. He won't be able to make it go up!"

"Good idea!" said the frog, and he tore off the handle. He put it into his mouth, for he was afraid to throw it anywhere in case the gnome found it again. He thought he would carry it a little way and then throw it into a bush. The fairy doll climbed on to his back, and held tight.

"Now please, don't be frightened," said the jumping frog. "I shall jump high, but you will be quite safe. I can't walk or run, you know."

"*I* shan't be frightened," said the fairy doll, clinging to his back. "I think you are the dearest, bravest, handsomest, strongest frog that I ever saw!"

Well! How Jinky swelled with pride when he heard that! He looked behind him to see that the gnome was still far away— but, oh my goodness, he was running back from his cottage at top speed, for he had seen the doll get out of the aeroplane!

Jinky wasted no more time but leapt high into the air and down again. Again and again he jumped, and each jump took him further away from the gnome, who had gone to his aeroplane to fly after them.

When he found that the starting handle had gone, he was very angry. He jumped out of the 'plane and ran to his garage. He opened the doors, and in a few moments Jinky heard the sound of a car engine roaring.

"Oh, my!" he thought in dismay. "If he comes after me in a car I shan't have any chance at all!"

On he went, leaping as far as he could each time. The fairy doll clung to him, and called to him to go faster still. Behind them came the gnome's car, driven at a fearful speed.

Then crash! There came a tremendous noise, and Jinky turned round to see what had happened. The gnome had driven so fast round a corner that he had gone smash into a tree, and his car was broken to pieces. Sly-One jumped out unhurt, very angry indeed. He shook his fist at the jumping frog, and looked at his broken car. Then he ran to a cottage nearby and thumped at the door.

The sleepy gnome came, and asked him what he wanted.

"Lend me your bicycle," demanded the gnome. "I want it to chase a wicked frog."

The goblin brought it out and the gnome jumped into the saddle. Off he pedalled at a furious rate after the frog and the doll.

"He's got a bicycle now!" shouted the fairy doll to Jinky. "Oh, hurry up, hurry up!"

Jinky jumped as fast as he could, but the doll was heavy and he began to be afraid that he would never escape. Behind him came the gnome on the bicycle, ringing his bell loudly all the time.

Suddenly the frog came to a village, and in the middle of the street stood a policeman with red wings. He held out his hand to stop Jinky and the doll, but with a tremendous jump the frog leapt right over him and was at the other end of the village before the angry policeman knew what had happened. Then he heard the loud ringing of Sly-One's bicycle bell, and turned to stop the gnome. He held out his hand sternly.

But the gnome couldn't and wouldn't stop! He ran right into the astonished policeman, and knocked him flat on his face. Bump! The gnome flew off his bicycle and landed right in the middle of the duck-pond nearby. The bicycle ran off by itself and smashed against a wall.

How angry that policeman was! He jumped to his feet and marched over to the gnome. "I arrest you for not stopping when I told you to, and for knocking me down," he said.

But the gnome slipped away from him, and ran down the street after the doll and the frog. The policeman ran after him, and off went the two, helter-skelter down the road.

The frog had quite a good start by now, and he was leaping for all he was worth. The doll was telling him all that had happened, and when he heard how the gnome had run into the policeman, he laughed so much that he got a stitch in his side and had to stop to rest.

"Oh, don't laugh!" begged the doll. "It really isn't funny. Do get on, Jinky."

His stitch was soon better, and on he went again, while some way behind him panted the gnome and the policeman. The frog felt sure he could jump faster than the gnome could run, so he wasn't so worried as he had been. For two more hours he jumped and jumped, and at last he came to the place where the toys had been dancing last night. They had all gone back to the nursery, very sad because they felt sure that the fairy doll and the frog were lost forever.

The frog jumped in at the window, and the fairy doll slid off his back. How the toys shouted and clapped their hands in glee! How they praised the brave frog, and begged his pardon for the unkind things they had said and done to him. And you should have seen his face when the fairy doll suddenly threw her arms round his neck and kissed him! He was so pleased that he jumped all round the room for joy.

Suddenly there was a shout outside. It was the gnome still running, and the policeman after him! The gnome was so angry that he meant to run into the nursery and fight the jumping frog!

Then the teddy bear did a clever thing. He put an empty box just underneath the window, and waited by it with the lid in his hands. The gnome jumped through the window straight into the box, and the bear clapped the lid down on him!

When the policeman came into the room too, the bear bowed gravely to him and handed him the box neatly tied round with string.

"Here is your prisoner," he said. "Please take him away, he is making such a noise."

The surprised policeman thanked the bear, bowed to the toys, and went out of the window again. Then the toys sat down and had a good laugh, but the one who laughed the loudest of all was Jinky, the little green frog!